M000196369

Showdown
at Snakegrass Junction

Also by Gary McCarthy:

THE DERBY MAN

Showdown
at Snakegrass Junction

GARY MCCARTHY

DOUBLEDAY & COMPANY, INC.

GARDEN CITY, NEW YORK

1978

First Edition

ISBN: 0-385-13689-7
Library of Congress Catalog Card Number 77–92223

Especially for Virginia

Showdown
at Snakegrass Junction

CHAPTER 1

Darby Buckingham eased his massive weight into the chair and studied the thin, aged face on the pillow. In sleep, Zeb Cather's expression was peaceful and the lines of pain soft. Darby touched the badge that rested on his own coat front. He desperately hoped to see it back on Zeb Cather's chest.

He ground the palms of his hands against his stinging, bloodshot eyes. He was sick of playing a lawman and, even worse, completely incompetent in the role. Just three nights before, he'd been involved in a gun fight. It was a miracle he was still alive.

Darby looked up and found Zeb Cather watching him. "You look whipped, man. That badge gets damned heavy, don't it?"

"I'll carry it until you're back on your feet and ready to strap your guns on again."

"Won't be long now, Darby. I'm feeling a little stronger every day. Just itching to get out of this bed. I've been a lawman for twenty-six years and an invalid for two months." His gray eyes drifted toward the window. "And believe me," he whispered, "the two months seems a lot longer than those twenty-six years."

"I've been thinking," Darby said, "about hiring a deputy."

The gray eyes jerked away from the window and Cather rasped, "No!"

"Why?"

"Well . . . well, it's a one-man job."

"If the man happens to be Zeb Cather rather than Darby Buckingham."

"Goddammit, that settles it!" the sheriff swore. "Out of the way. I'm taking over."

Darby grabbed him by the shoulders and gently pushed him down. In his weakened state, Zeb could offer no resistance.

"Buckingham," Zeb gasped, "I made you sheriff and I can take it away from you. You aren't going to hire no deputy!"

"We're reasonable men," Darby snapped. "So just lean back and tell me why."

Cather's mouth pinched tight. He was mad. Madder than hell.

Darby relaxed his grip. Take it easy, he told himself.

"The best reason I know is that the town budget can't afford it."

Darby sighed, and turned away. It was no reason at all. Darby had enough money to hire a dozen deputies right out of his own finances and Zeb knew it. The real reason was that Zeb didn't want a younger man to get a foothold in his office.

Darby nodded slowly. "You're right, I forgot about the budget. Why don't we forget I brought it up."

"Already forgotten," Zeb grumped.

A long, uncomfortable silence followed.

"What's bothering you, Zeb?" he finally asked. "You've been chewing at yourself for weeks."

"That noticeable, huh?"

"Yes," Darby said.

"You wouldn't believe me if I told you."

"Try me."

"There's trouble coming."

Darby leaned closer. "From where?"

"I don't know."

"Well, then, how—"

"I don't know how! That's why I knew you wouldn't believe me." He paused as though trying to choose his words carefully. "Look, you're a writer."

"So?"

"So you came clear from New York City to write a story about me. You didn't know me from Adam. You couldn't even have been sure I'd give you a story. But you came anyway. Why?"

"Well," Darby began, "I had a feeling—"

"Aha! You said it. Feeling. Or you could call it a hunch or an instinct. Whatever tag you put on it, it was so strong you came two thousand miles. What I'm trying to say is that I have the same feeling when it comes to sensing trouble. And I sense it now."

"Hmm," Darby mused. "You've had this feeling before and it was correct?"

"It's never failed me. The last time was before the bank holdup. And right now, it's three times as strong as then."

"What can I do? Do you have any suggested precautions?"

The older man shook his head. "That's what's chewing on me. I know it's coming but I don't know how or when. Driving me crazy!"

"Well, I'll just have to be extra careful."

"You been practicing with a gun like I showed you?"

"I rented a buckboard the day before yesterday and was going to practice, but—"

"Don't tell me the rest," Zeb groaned. "It was such a nice day you decided to take Miss Dolly Beavers along. Maybe have a big picnic. Right?"

Darby nodded sheepishly.

"And so you drove out and did about everything but what you were supposed to do in the first place."

"Blast!" Darby swore. "I'll never be any good with a gun and we both know it. A pen fits my hand, not a gun butt."

"Goddammit! That kind of thinking will get you buried."

"Any time," Darby said softly, "you want to pin this badge on another man you're welcome."

Zeb waved a hand and brushed the thought away. "You know I can't do it," he said. "The people around here wouldn't let me. They think you're John L. Sullivan and Wyatt Earp all rolled into one. I can see the Sullivan part, but I sure as hell can't see any Earp. I just wish you'd practice."

He looked up, an expression of defeat written across his weathered face. "By the way, how are you and Dolly getting along?"

"You're a nosy old devil, aren't you?"

"Well, when you get to be my age you'll find that about all you can do is talk about that sort of thing."

"What sort of thing?" Darby asked, watching Zeb squirm.

As was his custom when the conversation turned away from his liking, Zeb switched the subject. "I've *got* to get out of here. Another month of this and I won't know which end of a gun to stick in the holster."

Darby frowned. "You're worried about losing your skill. Will you?"

"I don't know," Zeb admitted. "Handling a six gun is something I've always done. Never been away from it this long. I have to practice. Trouble is coming, man! When it does I have to be able to stand up and face it. This is my town. They depend on me."

Darby turned away. He couldn't stand the look that Zeb wore. Maybe the legend of Cather was over—maybe not. But, whatever, Zeb needed time to heal. Darby meant to give him that time no matter what kind of trouble struck Running Springs.

"I won't let you fight my battles," Zeb said.

"Man, you have no choice!" Darby said as he tried to keep the exasperation from rising in his voice. "The doctor ordered you to stay in bed at least another month!"

The two iron-willed men exchanged glares. They were as different as snow and fire. Where the sheriff was long and spare, Darby appeared to be almost as wide as he was tall. He was an Easterner and wore a bulging frock coat, stiff white shirt, round-toed shoes, and his trade mark: an impeccably clean, shiny-banded, black derby hat.

He had almost no neck because of the powerful bunch of his shoulders. The mustache he wore was black and as thick as a slice of bacon. His arms filled the coat's sleeves like sausages. Darby stood five foot nine and appeared to be much shorter; probably it was because he tipped the scales at nearly 275 pounds. He had the girth of a horse. The shiny badge pinned against the expanse of his chest seemed the size of a small silver coin.

"You had a shooting three nights ago," the sheriff snapped accusingly.

"Just a couple of drunks that got a little overexuberant. Nothing serious."

"That's not what Dolly Beavers said. She told me you traded lead with them!"

Darby Buckingham gestured as if to shoo away a fly. "It was simply an unfortunate incident."

"Incident!" Zeb Cather roared, "Dolly said you fired twice and missed them both times. She says they were so drunk they ran out of bullets shootin' back at you."

"Well, I'll admit I'm not the best shot, but I was only trying to—"

"The best shot! You're no shot! You're going to get yourself into a corner and someone is going to gun you down."

Darby's eyes seemed to grow darker; his knuckles flattened over his clenched fists. "You seem to forget, Zeb, I tracked down and killed the man who shot you."

"I still don't know how you managed it," Cather said. "But it's true."

"Yes. And there's no sense going over it again. I don't like

this job, but, as you said yourself, no one else would take it."
His mustache bristled with annoyance; his eyes bored into
those of the old lawman. "Hurry up and get back on the job,
Zeb. I'm not suited for this role. And as you suggest, my in-
competence with a six gun is fast becoming legendary."

"So I've heard," the sheriff grinned. "Most of the people in
Running Springs feel the safest place to jump is the one
you're aiming at."

"An exaggeration!" Despite himself, Darby laughed.
"However, it has basis. The truth is that I'm a writer trying
to do a job ill suited to my abilities. But, in a month, when
you can properly fill your responsibilities as sheriff, I will be
delighted to return your badge. The pleasure will be all
mine."

"All right, Darby, but if there's trouble, gun trouble that
you have no business getting into, call me."

Darby stood up. "Just rest," he said, starting for the door,
feeling he'd won the argument.

"Wait," Zeb said quickly. "I— I just want to say thanks.
Thanks, and be careful. It's when a man's down that he's
gonna have trouble. After all these years, I can smell it coming."

Darby shrugged. "We can handle it, Sheriff. With your
gun, or," he added quickly, "my fists. We can handle it."

But late that evening as he made the rounds, hearing the old
boardwalk squeak and protest under his weight, Darby
wasn't so sure. Running Springs was, in the sheriff's words, a
magnet for violent men. Its visitors came from the mountains
and isolated ranches with unspent money in their pockets and
hell-raising in their hearts. The town was there to serve them,
entertain them. When their money was gone and their eyes
were bloodshot from whiskey and smoke, they would leave.
Businessmen would sigh with relief, count the change in their
tills, and gaze myopically out at the prairie, hoping to see another crowd gallop in.

Darby knew this time would soon pass. He was an Easterner born and raised. Though the Westerners did not believe it, he knew that someday the wildness of this country would be gone. The land would be drawn, quartered, and quartered again until it was no longer open and free. Cowboys would tend fences and stores. Big cities would mushroom until someday they would rival those of the East. As he crossed the street to peer into a bar, he had an undeniable sense of time passing. So it was that as each day ended he felt a growing restlessness to travel. It was his plan to write of the West, capture the times. He must, while it was still possible.

He stopped at the end of town and gazed out at sunset over the prairie. Slowly drawing a long Cuban cigar out of his pocket, he thought about his home. Despite his New York publisher's pleas that he return, Darby would not. He had the feeling that New York would always be there, solid, unchanging, while the West . . . the West was going through its wild, blood-pumping adolescence with a zest that could not last. But while it lasts, he thought, inhaling deeply from his cigar, I want to be here and watch. It should be quite a show.

A coyote howled. In moments, its lone call was echoed by a dozen others. It was a prairie chorus, a sagebrush symphony. Their song rolled upward until it resounded off the majestic Tetons and fell back at the town. The town answered with the sound of barroom laughter and piano music.

The night's activities were just beginning. He hoped it would prove quiet. The gun on his hip bunched clumsily under his black frock coat. He wore it high because his arms were short and heavily muscled. They were designed with power, but not speed. Darby smiled ruefully. His performance was ridiculous enough when he had the damn thing out; he shuddered at the thought of even attempting any semblance of a fast draw. He still had five toes on his right foot; he intended to keep them all. "I'm slow," he said aloud, "but I'm also a bad shot."

Chuckling at his own irony, he pulled his derby hat low

across his brow and reluctantly turned back toward town. The coyotes' howls receded behind him. At least they were in harmony with their surroundings. He wasn't. The sheriff's feeling for danger was something to respect. Trouble was a lawman's business. What the hell am I doing here? he wondered. And where would trouble come from next?

The two grizzled old frontiersmen sat tall and unmoving in their saddles as if they'd been hewn out of weather-beaten granite. They stared down at the settlement called Running Springs like hawks at a rabbit. On their lined, sun-scorched faces was a composite look of anger, contempt, and a grinning anticipation.

The shorter of the two was a thick-chested, fierce-looking man with a wild tangle of gray-streaked hair that exploded around the clamped edges of a mangy coonskin cap. His hair ran into a solid rug of deep black beard. As he glared down at the town below, he habitually and energetically scratched himself.

"Bear Timberly," his tall, sharp-faced companion said, "you must have brung every flea in Canada with you."

"For a fact," Bear grumbled. "Got a load of lice on my fur. It was a damn long winter. Hell, Zack, if you had any hair, I'd reckon you'd be itchin' too."

"Your mammy," Zack Woolsey replied softly, "she musta been a gawdamn sow-bear."

"Go to hell," came a rumbling reply. He hesitated a moment. "But I sure wouldn't turn down a real hot-water bath." He suddenly jerked his hand up and under his leather shirt. "One hot enough to boil these little bloodsuckers!" Bear swore and pulled a louse out and held it up in front of his eyes. With a triumphant look, he crushed it between his pickle-thick thumb and forefinger.

Zack Woolsey laughed, and the tightness in his face disappeared. He was on the sundown side of sixty, but he carried himself like a young man—straight and strong. Like his partner, Zack was dressed in buckskins, dark-stained with blood. He wore moccasins, but, instead of a coonskin, he favored a wide-brimmed, colorless felt hat. At six foot four, he stood out in a crowd.

His hair and beard were silver, but thin, as he was. He shifted the Sharps buffalo rifle in the crook of his arm and spit a long, mean streak of tobacco juice at Running Springs.

"It's places like that 'un," Zack said, "made us go north into Canada these last few years. Makin' us freeze every winter to earn a living!"

Bear nodded. "The cold seems to bite deeper each trip. Still, we made good money this time, Zack."

"Yeah, yeah, we did. Seven hundred dollars ain't bad for two old men, I reckon. But we're havin' to go farther north each year to do it." His voice dropped. "This winter even my bones felt frozen. And remember . . . remember how it used to be out there?" he asked, sweeping a long arm before them. "Before that town ruined it? How many years did we trap in this valley together? How many!" he demanded.

"Fifteen, eighteen years. A chunk. I remember, the antelope and buffalo used to trip over theirselves when we first came into this country. Now they're 'most gone," Bear concluded wistfully.

"Yeah, only, 'cept now we got people. People crawling all over the place. Why, there must be a hundred down there!"

"Probably more."

"If I'd have seen how it was going to be," Zack said squeezing his rifle, "I'd have sided with the Injuns again' my own people."

"They ain't our people."

"You're right."

"You want to level 'er?"

"Be right fittin'," Zack said. "Do you think we could?"

"Sure. Ain't no town has enough law to stand up to the likes of us."

"That's what you said just before we rode into Denver year before last."

"Different thing altogether!" Bear protested. "Hell, they had lawmen crawling all over the place. Musta been at least half a dozen. This town can't have more than a couple. Besides, Zack, you forgetting what we did that time in Cody?"

"That was a long while back. Things are changing too fast for the likes of us."

"You sayin' we're too old to tame a town?" Bear asked in astonishment.

"Naw, I ain't saying that atall."

"Then let's go . . . unless yore scared."

Zack Woolsey punched straight from the shoulder. His long arm shot out and sent his bony knuckles into the side of Bear's head. The punch had enough force to stun.

Bear blinked, then squinted his eyes. "Damn you, Zack," he said in a rising voice, "you set my ears to ringing again!"

In answer, he was splattered by a stream of tobacco juice. It soaked into his buckskin shirt.

Bear stared down at the slippery puddle in disbelief. Suddenly he exploded. "That's it! You got me riled, Zack! I ain't shook your tree in more'n a week now and you're ripe for a beatin'!" He reined his horse viciously, trying to get into arm's reach. But Zack Woolsey, anticipating Bear's move, as always, kicked Bear in the side, almost unseating him. Then he swung his horse around and drove his heels against the animal's ribs, forcing it into a gallop. His voice carried high and happy. "Come on, old Bear, we are overdue for some hell-raising!"

CHAPTER 2

Darby Buckingham lay stretched on his hotel-room floor. His face was set in grim determination as he adjusted his powerful shoulders flat against the carpet and gripped the end of the brass bedstead. He could feel a shifting of the bed from above. "Are you *sure* you're ready this time, Miss Beavers? Yesterday, you lost your balance up there and I still feel as if you cracked my ribs when you landed on my chest."

"Just a moment, dear," Dolly Beavers called down sweetly.

Darby sighed and wondered what was taking her so long. Suddenly, her face loomed into view. She had a nice face. It was round and sweet and encircled by curly blond hair. The fact that it was a little too round didn't bother him in the least. He was robust and he liked a woman to be the same. Dolly had everything a man could want.

"Darby, honey, I'll do my best, and I've already explained about how the accident happened yesterday. This time, I promise to hold on tight. No more leaning over to watch."

"Good!" he answered with a sense of relief. "And if you feel yourself falling, at least don't you *and* the trunk land on me. Okay, I'm set. This is the heaviest weight I've lifted yet, and I may be a bit unsteady, so hang on!"

Dolly's face disappeared as she took her position. "I'm ready if you are. Sure is high up here, though. It'd be a long fall."

Darby ignored her remark, readjusted his grip, and began to take a series of deep breaths in rapid succession. The fast breathing was a trick he'd learned as a circus strong man—

that, and total concentration. When attempting any great feat of strength, he'd found the idea was to put his mind completely against the obstacle to be overcome, then act fast.

Suddenly his entire body knotted and, with a low growl, he flashed power through his shoulders and into his arms. The arms were capable of the task. They shuddered, corded, and very slowly, they straightened. The solid brass rails creaked in protest and, high above, the heavy-filled wooden trunk and Dolly Beavers, by no means a slight woman, began to rise. Darby Buckingham glared with bright black eyes at the weight. His lips were drawn flat against his teeth and his grin was triumphant. Then, as his arms locked, he expelled a great whoosh of air, and the bed eased down.

"Darby, honey, you did it!"

"Of course," he replied matter-of-factly. "If you'll hang on until I'm finished, I will attempt this feat nine more times."

Dolly Beavers bubbled. "I'll count for you. Start when you're ready. Just wait until the girls hear about this!"

"Forget the girls. Here goes."

Again the bed rose steadily upward, hung trembling for a moment, then descended with her count, "Two, three, four, five. Oh, you're so strong!"

His arms filled with a marrow-core pain. His neck sunk, turtle-like, deep into his chest, and his eyes squeezed almost shut. Sweat popped out on his face and he ground his teeth and glared at the bloodless hands, willing them to raise the weight four more times. It was heavier than he'd expected. Forget the pain, think of the weight as an enemy to be conquered. You can do it. Concentrate!

On six, Darby's attention was broken by a tremendous crash against the wall not eight feet from where he lay. The bed swayed drunkenly. A picture with glass fell and shattered. He tried to ignore it and forced the bed upward again.

"Oh, damn!" Dolly swore. "Seven!" She shifted anxiously atop the trunk. "Those two old devils! I never should have rented them a room."

The bed swayed precariously. "Sit still, Miss Beavers!" Darby gasped, fighting to control the weight that balanced at arm's length. "Only two m-more."

"Eight."

Two more, he thought grimly. I can do it. He bunched his shoulders, screwed his chin into his chest and heaved. The bed seemed reluctant to leave the floor; it gave ground like a piker. This time, it fought his arms every inch of the way up. His breath whistled through his teeth.

"Hurry, Darby. They'll ruin the place."

An angry roar cut through the wall. "I'm going to drown you, Zack. I—" The words were sliced short by a loud splintering of wood. A cry of hurt indignation followed.

Dolly had forgotten the count. "How could I have been so stupid! They're going to destroy that room!"

The bed was at arm's length and, almost out of control, swinging like a pendulum. "Please," he gasped.

"I've got to do something, Darby. I can't just sit here like a hen on eggs."

The bed dropped down almost out of control. It lit on one leg, then thudded to rest. "Nine," he wheezed. "Once more, that's all I ask. Now, sit still!"

"OK! Nine, dammit."

Under the bed, Darby Buckingham hesitated, shocked by the ire in her voice. That wasn't like her at all; he'd never heard Dolly Beavers lose her temper. "Almost finished. Here we go."

The bed had barely started up when something hit the wall so hard the plaster cracked. Darby set the bed down and felt Dolly move above. "If you remain seated just a couple seconds more I'll accompany you next door. Try to understand that I said I would lift you, the chest and this bed—all of it— ten times. So I must!"

Her voice was nervous and carried a measure of anxiety to him. "All right, but hurry," she shouted. "This is torture.

And to think I gave them the John C. Fremont Suite because they said they were explorers!"

"The John C. Fremont Suite? You mean room 211?"

"Of course. You see, many years ago, Mr. Fremont—"

A cry interrupted them. "Bear, no more. I can't swim!"

"Good!"

Up on the trunk, he heard Dolly moan. Darby gulped a quick, deep breath and wrenched at the bed with dead arms. The bed stayed put. Another, deeper breath. "Ahhh!" he roared in challenge. This time, the bed broke from the floor. "Ahhh!" he shouted again, and the bed went higher.

"Look out!" came a cry through the wall, "you're turning the whole thing over! Bear, don't do it!"

The answering response was immediate. "You've lived too long anyways, Zack Woolsey."

A tremendous crash shook the top floor of the Antelope Hotel and was followed by the second of a cascading waterfall. Dolly Beavers let out a bellow and vaulted erect. Her feet sank into the high, tilting mattress as she struggled for balance.

"Dolly!" Darby screeched, his arms pumping like pistons as first one side of the bed, then the other, drove down at him. "I can't hold it with—"

It was too much. The bed tilted wildly to the left, hung for one awful, menacing second, then collapsed, hurling upwards of four hundred pounds at the floor. Dolly Beavers, tottering near the ceiling, flipped high into the air. The massive, book-laden trunk ponderously rolled and dropped. Dropped on Darby's stomach.

A great whoosh of air escaped from his lips and a hot, red explosion blossomed before the writer's eyes. He was aware, just when the pain was the greatest, that Dolly Beavers crashed over the trunk, and it seemed to drop through him.

He lay sick and gasping like a beached whale. Darby Buckingham was sure he was going to die.

A voice, far away, echoed in his brain. "Darby, Darby, I'm sorry!"

His eyes fluttered weakly and he felt the wetness of tears dropping on his face.

Dolly was shoving at the trunk with all her considerable strength. It rolled off his stomach and crunched onto his arm. "Ahhh!"

"Oh!" she cried in horror, and he felt the trunk being moved again. Will it never, he thought hazily, come to rest?

She buried his face. She pressed out his air. With the strength of a dying man, he shoved her. "You're . . . you're smothering me, Miss Beavers!" he croaked. "And . . . and let loose of my head, you're . . . you're bending my ears!"

She was bawling; she made great, wolfing noises of such intensity he forgot his own sense of dying. "Forgive me!"

He managed to nod, and with a cry of happiness she smothered his face again. Too weak to move, he was spared imminent suffocation by a piercing scream that told him he was not the only departing soul in the Antelope Hotel.

Then a fist drove through the wall. Darby saw it emerge just over his bureau. It jammed back and forth in frantic haste, unable to withdraw.

"My God!" Dolly gasped, staring at the wiggling fingers. "I've got to stop them before they level the entire floor!"

Darby Buckingham tried to raise himself on one elbow. She pushed him back. "No, no! You're hurt and you look sort of pasty white. I'll go myself. You lie still," she soothed, rising up and starting for the door.

"Dolly!"

"Yes?"

"Please retrieve the washbasin before you leave; I feel sick."

She spun around and raced across the room. Snatching his heavy white porcelain washbasin, she ran back to him. At that moment, the hand disappeared and Darby saw a face. Then it was gone, leaving a huge hole.

"Oh, damn you!" Dolly wailed. "Here," she said, extending the basin as she whirled for the door, murder burning in her usually placid blue eyes.

Weakly he reached for it—but not fast enough. His fingers brushed the bowl, then it dropped like a stone and bounced squarely off his forehead.

Dolly Beavers, however, didn't see it shatter, didn't hear Darby's oath or watch his eyes roll upward; she was already flying out the door.

Inside the John C. Fremont Suite, they were stark naked. The ponderous Bear Timberly was saddled atop the overturned bathtub. In one hand, he gripped an ornamental iron tub leg, in the other a bottle of whiskey. Underneath him, the tub was moving, as a scrambling pair of knees and hands propelled it back and forth in frantic, crab like bursts.

"Git up, hoss! Ya! Ya!" Bear roared, drumming his bare heels against the tub's sides.

"I'm gonna kill you, I git outa here," Zack Woolsey shrieked from inside the tub, the echoes bouncing at him.

"You had to be the first in the bath, didn't ya!" Bear laughed, kicking the tub even harder. "You wanted all the hot water—wanted it first so's I wouldn't leave any lice and dirt in it!" He smiled down triumphantly. "Well, I reckon next time you'll know who comes first in this partnership. Yaah! Yaah! Git moving, Zack!" Bear yelled, whipping the overturned tub with his whiskey bottle.

"Open up! Open up in there!" Dolly Beavers screamed from the hallway. "Or I'll let myself in!"

Inside the room it became quiet. Then a voice answered, "You'll have to wait, ma'am, until we can git some clothes on."

"And let you wreck even more? Not on your worthless lives, I won't," she swore, flashing her pass key. In a matter of seconds, she was barreling through the doorway. She was stopped dead in her tracks by what she saw. Bear was half way into his leather breeches, while Zack Woolsey had one leg sticking free from under the tub and was coming out—until he saw Dolly.

She blanched at the sight. Shock gave way to rage. Bear began to dance around on one foot, trying to get the other to go through the empty leg hole in his pants. The one under the tub peeked out like a gray snail. Dolly whirled toward him and the tub dropped back down, covering him like a shell.

Bear finally got his second leg through the pants. "Ma'am, you shouldn't have come barging in here like that," he grumbled. "Hell, this is our room, we paid for it!"

"To use!" Dolly raged, "not to destroy! Now, I want you and that idiot under the tub to get dressed and git!"

The tub again lifted. She remembered the man's name was Zack.

"I'm no idiot, lady," he grunted, "and we ain't gonna be thrown out. I intend to get me a bath one way or another!"

Dolly glared at them. "You crazy old goats! Just look at this place! You've destroyed the washstand, ruined my rugs, put a hole in my walls, and now, now you stand almost naked before a decent woman and tell her you're wanting a bath! Is that what you're saying? Do I understand you?" she yelled, marching forward.

Bear retreated to the far wall. He glanced over at Zack for help, but his partner had ducked back under the iron tub. Bear glared defensively at her. She stood her ground and glared right back. His eyes dropped.

"Well," he stuttered, "we did pony up two dollars for the room. And as for the damage, we'd be glad to pay on our way out, I—"

"Good, then pay me now! 'Cause, mister, you and your friend are on the way out!"

He seemed to rumble up from deep inside. Dolly saw the tendons expand against his neck.

"No!" he spat. He advanced on her. "We paid, I said."

Dolly, suddenly unsure, began backing up. "Are you going?" she spluttered, retreating to the door.

"When I'm ready! *That's* when! Right now, we want more water."

"Then, go jump in the horse tank!"

"I said more water!"

Dolly had her hand on the doorknob now, and she backed into the hall hissing, "You'll git no water, either of you. If you must, then roll around in what you've spilled on the floor, just like the pigs you are!"

He reared back and bashed another hole in her wall. "If you weren't a woman, why, I'd . . ."

"You'd do exactly the same," she blazed, "nothing! I'll tell you something else. You better be packed and gone within five minutes or I'll return with Mr. Darby Buckingham, whose room adjoins this one. He's already madder'n hell because you put your stupid fist through his wall. He's big and strong and he'll throw you both out the window!"

"Oh, yeah?"

"Yeah!"

"Ain't a single man alive could throw Bear Timberly and Zack Woolsey out a window." A curious expression crossed his face. Then he smiled. "Hell, lady, you just go an' bring him on; we'll tear down his meat house right before your eyes!"

"All right," Dolly said, compressing her words into a tight angry, clipped sound. "We'll see! I'll bring him back in just fifteen minutes. But, for the sake of your own worthless hides, I hope you're outta here!"

Dolly slammed the door. She felt her heart race, and her knees felt ready to buckle. She backed up against the hallway and bit her knuckles. How could she have been so stupid as to rent them the room? Thank heavens, she thought, for her man, Darby Buckingham. Well, no matter what he did to those two, they deserved it. Just wait until she told him what they'd said.

Darby Buckingham felt the cold water being splashed on his face. He woke up feeling mashed.

"Darby . . . Darby . . . what did you do to yourself? Your forehead, it's—"

"You dropped the—"

"Oh, never mind," she rushed, "there's these two old men next door. They're the ones who were making such a noise. Anyway, they *refused* to vacate the John C. Fremont Suite! That's when I told them you would come over and throw them out. Oh, Darby, they've destroyed the room."

He avoided her eyes. His fingers reached up to examine the knot on his forehead. Oh, God, he thought, I'm going to look like a unicorn.

"Darby, did you hear me?"

"Yes, yes, I think so. So what?"

"So what! So, are you going to do it?"

Darby groaned and pushed himself up onto his elbows. "Really, Miss Beavers, I don't believe I am physically capable of throwing anyone, even two old men, out of anything. Why don't you go downstairs and hire someone to do the job?"

He saw disbelief cross her face. She actually recoiled. He saw an image crumble in her eyes, turn to dust. Darby blinked and reached out for her. Her arm, when he grasped it, was rigid. Her lips formed words less than a whisper. "Are you . . . are you afraid?"

Darby lay back until his head rested on the floor. He stared at the ceiling. It seemed to rotate from above. He'd been hit hard enough in his prize-fighting days to know he needed time. He closed his eyes. "No, I'm not afraid of them."

"Darby, I'm sorry," she said moving close. "It's just that

. . . well, I told them about you. And I didn't want them to think you're a chicken-heart."

He looked up at her. His vision was almost back to normal. "Go get me a cigar and pour me a double shot of my brandy. Right now, please."

She seemed puzzled, but his gaze was even and determined. Moments later, she returned.

The cigar was long and black and expensive. Darby Buckingham sighed contentedly while she held the match. He inhaled deeply. "These Cuban cigars put our own native tobaccos to shame, you know," he said, studying the cigar intently.

"That's all very good," Dolly said coldly, "but what about—"

"The two old men?"

"Yes."

Darby glanced at the hole in the wall. He took a hefty swallow of brandy and felt it drop warmly along the front of his backbone. "It seems to me, in order to do that kind of damage they can't be too old. Are you sure you're not setting me up for a thrashing?"

"Why, no! I wouldn't want you to get hurt."

He pursed his lips thoughtfully. "No, I can't believe that you would. I mean, I really don't see what you'd gain by it. Except perhaps. . . ."

"What?"

"So you'd have me stuck here in bed so I couldn't leave town."

She blushed. "Oh, Darby, you are such a suspicious man."

"A writer has to be suspicious," he said dryly. "And right now, I'm wondering how an old man could possibly have put his fist through the wall and raised all that racket. Besides, they've quieted. Maybe they'll be on their best behavior the—"

There was a powerful hammering on the wall. "Our fifteen

minutes are up. What's keeping that dude that was gonna throw us out the window?"

An expression of great pain slipped over Darby's round face. "You told them I was going to toss them out the window?"

"Well, they—"

He shook his head in resignation. "You did tell them. Now they're mad, and they want to fight."

"So what?" Dolly snapped. "They've almost wrecked the place! I'd fight them myself if I was a man. What's wrong with you, anyway? You lift weights, you were a circus strong man, and once an undefeated prize fighter."

"Nothing is wrong, except that I don't intend to throw anyone out of windows, and I don't feel up to a fight. To be perfectly honest, right at this moment, I'd prefer to lie here and smoke this cigar and drink enough brandy to subdue the pain just inflicted on me by you. Besides, I'm not so young that I brawl for the fun of it."

Dolly snorted disgustedly. "Oh, hell-fire! You're not much older than me and I haven't hit forty yet."

"But I'm wiser than you, my dear," Darby replied. "I know enough to stay out of trouble unless trouble troubles me. And those men next door aren't troubling me."

"If you don't . . ." Bear's voice cut through the ragged hole, ". . . git over here to throw us out our window, we're coming over to throw you outa yours!"

Dolly smiled sweetly. "As you were saying, love?"

"Help me up," he groaned.

Darby staggered over to the mirror to study the monument that was growing on his forehead. The head ached and so did his muscles from lifting the four hundred-odd pounds ten times. That, and his stomach felt as if it were going to start doing an acrobatic act of its own.

He took a deep swallow of brandy to try to console all of

his pains at once. "All right, I'll go and see what can be done with them. But you wait here!" he ordered, punching the long cigar into his mouth. "Just in case there is an irreconcilable difference to be resolved."

Dolly smiled and blew him a kiss. "When they see what a big, strong man you are, they'll be stumbling all over each other trying to get out of the John C. Fremont Suite. You just wait and see, Darby. 'Bye, now!"

CHAPTER 3

Darby stood hesitating outside Room 211. Inside, he couldn't hear a sound. What would they be up to? God only knows, he thought. They sound crazy enough to shoot me. For a moment, he considered going back to his room and getting a gun. He rejected the idea as overreacting. Besides, they might mistake his intent and go for their own weapons. No, he decided, at worst he could physically remove them. At best, they might respond to reason and go peaceably.

They were probably drunk. There could be no other excuse for their wild behavior. He bristled when he thought about the hole in his wall. Well, he thought, hitching up his pants, they'd pay for that before they left.

He heard a door squeak and twisted around to see Dolly peeking at him. "Well," she whispered, "what are you waiting for?"

"Would you go back and wait! Woman, let me handle this my way."

Dolly looked like she was going to argue, but Darby scowled so darkly she retreated. He waited until the door clicked shut, and then he turned back to Room 211. Still no sound.

They're going to waylay me, he thought. Darby puffed quickly on the cigar, frowning with concentration. He had a stomach ache right where the trunk had landed. He felt lousy. But they didn't care. So it was just a matter of overpowering two lunatics.

But lunatics could be the most dangerous kind. Suppose

they were waiting with weapons trained on the doorway? What would Zeb Cather do?

Zeb would kick the door in and jump sideways. That's what I'll do, Darby decided. And he did.

The door crashed inward, Darby leapt sideways. No gunfire, no sound. What the hell? He peeked around the corner and saw a huge man, a very hairy man. The man smiled.

Darby frowned. He felt a little ridiculous. "My name is Darby Buckingham," he said.

"Mine's Bear Timberly. I've heard plenty about you and it's a pleasure to shake your hand."

Darby scratched the knot on his forehead quizzically. He looked down at the proffered hand and took it.

The instant flesh touched flesh, he knew he'd made a big mistake. Bear's fist clamped onto his own and the man yanked him off his feet and into the room. He tripped on a tangle of animal traps and slipped on the wet floor.

He tried to free his hand, but Bear's grip had the tenacity of a pit-bull. A wild cry erupted from behind him and Darby twisted halfway around to see a gray-bearded, tree-tall man leap from behind the doorway.

A long, looping blow caught him behind the ear. Darby felt his knees sag. Next, the tall one whipped a left uppercut from somewhere near ankle level. It caught Darby just under the ribs and blasted him back into the hallway. He crashed against the wall.

Bear was on him instantly. Those powerful hands grabbed Darby by the shirt front and, with a tremendous heave, threw him back into the room. In that instant, Darby knew he'd met a man with strength to match his own. Darby hit the carpet and rolled.

"Close the door, Zack; we don't want anyone to see this dude toss us out the window."

Darby was on the floor, his face pressed into the wet rug. Slowly, he rubbed his hand in the water and then wiped his face. His eyes were almost closed, but if Bear or Zack could have seen them, they might have finished him right then and there.

"Look at that!" Zack said; "our guest musta forgot to wash his face before comin' over to visit us."

Darby ignored them. Let them come to him when they were through with their fun; he needed every second he could get. Hell of a way to go into a fight, he thought.

He shook his head slowly, then elbowed himself over on his back to glare at them.

"Jeezus! Would you look at that lump," Zack swore. "Musta bruised his brains, else he wouldn't even have come over here."

Darby pushed himself to his feet and retreated a few faltering steps until his back was against the wall. They seemed to be waiting for him to speak. That's what they wanted. His eyes went from one to the other, and he said nothing. It occurred to him that he faced a very different breed of animal in these two. It wouldn't be a stand-up, square-off, fist fight. He was in for an all-out, eye-gouging, cat fight. They'd know tricks he'd never thought of.

When they charge, he decided, I'm going to hit the shorter one squarely in the throat. If it kills him, well, it can't be helped. They are both too big and too strong to take chances with—especially the thick, hairy one. As Darby thought of Dolly referring to them as 'two old men,' his face took on a bitter cut of amusement.

The moments dragged by in silence, and the two rugged frontiersmen's eyes never left him. What the devil are they waiting for? Darby wondered. Didn't they realize time was to his advantage? He discarded the idea. It wouldn't even have occurred to them. He was sure they were, at best, only amused by him. Two rangy and scarred alley cats watching a cornered mouse squirm. A smile crossed under Darby's mustache.

"What the thunder you grinnin' about?" Zack demanded.

Darby drew in a deep breath and balled his fists at his sides. Might as well get this over with. "I've written stories about mangy characters, but you're a pair that puts them to shame."

"That was an insult, Zack!"

"I know, I know. But what I don't know is why he's doin' it."

Darby was surprised. Perhaps he'd misjudged the man. Despite appearance, Darby thought, the tall one is a thinker. Perhaps even a reasonable man. "You have a choice," he said, "pay damages and leave town or you're under arrest."

Bear took a draft of his bottle, his eyes bright with anticipation. "We paid fair money for this room, mister. We ain't leavin' it, by the window or otherwise. You ain't got the same choice."

Darby's thick black mustache lifted slightly at the corners of his mouth. "You're leaving town," he said softly, "because you put a hole in my wall, and I didn't like your welcome surprise."

Zack chuckled. "First time I ever heard of a wallopin' called a surprise." His eyes narrowed. "I admire you for still being able to stand up. But I didn't try to break you in half."

"That's a comfort to know; still, it hurt."

"Yep, just enough to take the pepper out and still not gut you."

"Your mistake, I'm afraid. Now nothing short of an apology and your immediate departure from this room will suffice. And payment for damages, of course. What I ought to do is arrest you both."

"You're speakin' to Bear Timberly, mister. Better shut up before I git me mad."

Darby leaned easily against the wall. "Go ahead, Bear Timberly. Get just as mad as you please. It changes nothing."

Bear took another long drink, his face hard, eyes dilating with an anger that spelled destruction. "You stay put, Zack; he's mine!"

Darby Buckingham got ready. The aching in his arms, the throbbing in his head were forgotten; he wasn't even aware of the numbness in his forearm where the trunk had landed on it. As he waited for the charge, it occurred to him that if his life had been different, if he'd been born earlier and on the frontier, he would have been much like this man before him. The courage and pride in Bear Timberly was a thing he could understand; that, and the total absence of hesitation to fight when you knew your capabilities and a man gave you no choice.

"Have you ever been beaten?" Darby asked. "I want to know if this will be the first."

Bear just laughed, but it wasn't a fun laugh. It was half angry and half wild, and it sent shivers down Darby's back. Then Bear charged, and his fist swept in like a mallet.

Darby crouched and shoved off from the wall, his own knuckles cutting a mean arc that exploded into the man's ribs. Bear's face seemed to expand and Darby leaned back and drove a straight left jab that connected squarely on the side of the jaw. Bear's face slammed into the wall and when he turned, the disbelief overrode the pain.

"Pay the damages," Darby said quietly, "then leave town."

Bear looked at his friend, and Darby saw a moment of shamed apology in his eyes.

"Bear?" Zack asked tentatively.

"Uh-uh, stay put." He blinked at Darby. "You got in a lucky first punch and you hit a wallop, mister. But that's it!"

This time, Bear didn't even bother to swing. He came straight on, and he took a jolting shot to the forehead, but his terrible momentum drove Darby to the wall, pinning his arms to his sides. For a moment they stood locked and straining, two men closely matched and endowed with enormous strength. Then, all at once, Bear let go and grabbed Darby by the flesh on his sides.

A cry rose in Darby's throat and he hammered a fist into Bear's eyes. Once, twice, while his own pain threatened to choke his mind. The talons unsnapped and Bear threw out a leg and tripped him hard. A split second later, a foot swept in and caught Darby under the jaw, snapping his head up. He rolled on instinct and saw Bear crash to the floor with drawn knees.

Darby twisted and lashed out blindly, and felt the pain of knuckles biting flesh. He saw Bear fall away. Darby hoped the fight was about over, yet knew better. Bear Timberly was bloodied and his eyes were swelling shut fast. But he wasn't finished.

Bear shook his head back and forth, he was on his hands and knees, and Darby watched him struggle to stand. Before he could find his balance, Darby was after him on the lunge. He sent a punch into Bear's face that flipped him over, shaking the room when he fell. Darby waited, then Bear started to crawl up again.

"Oh, gawdammit," Zack cried brokenly. "I can't stand it!" With a wild, climbing war whoop, he sprang into action.

"Zack, no!" Bear spat. But it was too late.

A whiskey bottle can crack a man's skull. Zack brought it down like a club. There were tears in his eyes, and that saved Darby's life; the bottle just grazed the back of his head and he twisted, intent on only one thing—to kill Zack Woolsey. He got his hands around the tall man's neck. Zack tripped him and they went down fighting. Darby's superior strength prevailed and he came upon top. Now it was his turn! But, somehow, Bear managed to reach them. His weight knocked Darby over and they rolled, punching.

Darby found himself astride Bear while Zack Woolsey was pounding his back. Whiskey splashed over him and he knew

Zack was trying to get the bottle up high enough to whack him a second time. Darby reached over his shoulder with one hand and got a fistful of Zack's long hair. He yanked it down hard and the man hollered as he bowled over and spilled across the floor with the bottle still in his hand. And right then, Zack did a peculiar thing; he tok a long slug off the bottle and brayed like a mule, while Darby, momentarily distracted, took a bone-jarring punch from Bear Timberly.

For a second, Darby's eyes began to glaze; it was the first really solid punch Bear had been able to land and it almost took his head off. He'd been lucky so far, but now he must try to take Bear out while his luck held, and before the tall, crazy one stopped laughing. Darby blocked another punch and drove both hands down until he had two fistfuls of Bear's wild, gray-black mane, then he yanked the head off the floor and smashed it down, as hard as he could, once, twice, and more. Bear stopped fighting.

Zack Woolsey charged. The bottle was still in his hand. When Darby saw him start to swing, he dodged sideways. But he'd underestimated the tall one. At the last moment, Darby realized he'd been tricked. He tried to avoid the blow, caught a glimpse of the whiskey splashing downward. He was too late and off balance. Darkness fell like a black shroud and spun him into insensibility.

Next door, Dolly Beavers was pacing the floor in nervous agitation. There had been no sound from the John C. Fremont Suite for several long minutes. Had Darby killed them? Maybe he'd really gotten mad and had thrown them both out on the street. Quickly she went to Darby's window, tossed back the curtains, and looked out. No, she couldn't see any bodies. And there would be a crowd, too. She breathed a sigh of relief; he must have knocked them out. Should she go and see? He had ordered her to wait; waiting, though, was unbearable.

Dolly straightened her dress before the mirror. She still had a good figure, maybe a few more pounds than she once had, but Darby himself had said he liked her ample. She hurriedly brushed her dark blond hair into place and started for the door. She was just about to place her hand on the doorknob when it turned. "Oh, Darby," she exclaimed, grabbing the handle.

"He can't hear a sweet-lovin' word you're sayin'." Bear grinned, wincing from a split lip as he did so. "Move aside, lady; he's heavy as hell and we can't stand here holding him like this all day."

"If you've killed him, I swear I'll shoot you both!" Before they could get him to the bed, Dolly threw herself at Darby. Bear and Zack dropped him heavily to the floor and staggered back as Dolly fell on top of him and hugged the writer's face tightly to her breast. She began to rock his head violently under her weight. A gagging sound could be heard.

"We didn't kill your boyfriend," Zack said, "but *you're* sure as hell gonna if you don't uncover his face, lady."

Dolly recoiled and found Darby's face had deepened to a pale blue color. She drew her hand to her lips in fear.

"He'll be okay, ma'am. Just needs airing out some." Bear shrugged. "But tell me. You didn't mean that—whatcha said?"

"What did I say?"

"You know. About shooting Zack and me."

"Damn right I did! How did you do this?"

"Wasn't easy," Zack admitted. "He's a heller in a fight."

Dolly stared wetly into Darby Buckingham's battered face. "Oh," she said, biting her lips, "I'm so sorry. But don't you worry, love; Dolly will take care of you."

The two old frontiersmen shifted uneasily. Zack poked a finger in his ear and began scratching it for nothing better to do. "I purely hated to poleax him with a bottle. But there didn't seem to be much else, short of shootin' him, when he charged. Murder was in his eyes. "Now," he said, smoothly switching the subject, "about that room, ma'am?"

She glanced up in disbelief. "Hang the room! You two are going to help me get Darby to bed Now! Or so help me, I'm going to get my gun and blow you both all over my hallway carpets!"

"All right! Don't udder up, ma'am. Take it slow," Bear pleaded. "Here, move away and we'll carry him, easy as a babe, inside."

They dropped him onto the mattress; he was still out cold. Zack looked at Dolly and combed his hair with his fingers. "Say, lady, he's going to be asleep for a long time yet and you ain't ugly. Bear and me would be proud to have you join us in a party. We could go over to the saloon, maybe do a little dancin', even!"

"You're crazy, both of you!" Dolly took a step back and her blue eyes shuttered. "But I'd like to see you dance, all right."

"Ya would?"

"Yes, at the end of a rope!"

Bear Timberly was taken aback. "Oh, lady, you can't mean that! Why, we're real sorry about bustin' up them little things in our room. And as for the bath water, why, that ain't nothing to fret your pretty self over. Hell-fire! the water is already startin' to seep down through the cracks, so it'll be dry almost before you know it."

Her expression forced his eyes to the floor. But only for an instant. When he looked up, she saw him glance at his friend and wink.

"Tell you what, ma'am; if you was to join us, we'd give the bath another try. You couldn't hardly do no better, ma'am."

Dolly reared back and swung; her fist connected solidly, and Bear cupped his nose with both hands and ground his teeth in pain. "That's my answer," she hissed, feeling a sense of triumph. She'd met their kind before, though not for years. There was only one thing they understood: force. Dolly balled her fists. In that moment, she felt as though nothing could stop her. She hated them!

"Whoa up, lady, we've had enough fighting for one day," Zack said. He turned to Bear. "I think we'd better leave."

At the door, Zack hesitated, "I like a woman with your spirit. You have a change of mind, you know where you can find me. And don't worry about Bear, here; he'd understand how you'd favor me."

"The hell she does!" Bear swore from the hallway.

"The hell she don't!"

Suddenly the hand of Bear Timberly appeared, and Zack was lifted out of the doorway and there was a wild squeal, then a thud followed by a crash. When Dolly grabbed the doorknob, she caught a glimpse of the two half-clad buffalo hunters rolling around on the floor screaming, spitting, and gouging. She slammed the door, leaned back against it and felt them bounding off the hall walls. "Please, God," she whispered, "don't let them roll down the stairs into the lobby. There'd be nothing left for me to save."

CHAPTER 4

Dolly Beavers sat on the bed and worried about Darby Buckingham. There was an angry swelling between his eyes that was rising faster than a bowl of yeast dough for tomorrow's bread. It was her fault, she knew, that he had gotten knocked unconscious. If she intended to keep him in Running Springs, she had better see that no more of this happened.

She studied his room. The shelves of books on the west wall reminded her again that he was a writer. She smiled with pride. Darby was the leading dime novelist of the day. Once, when they had sipped brandy longer than usual, he had admitted as much. Why, he'd even brought out copies of some of his books. Dolly remembered how she'd laughed at the exaggerated depictions of screaming Indians and terrible-faced badmen carrying off the heroine, with the hero in hot pursuit. And the titles! They had both laughed at them—*Singing Six Guns* and *Lightning Guns*, with the cover displaying something resembling bolts of lightning shooting from the twin barrels in the hands of a snow-white-clad hero. But the one called *The Legend of Zeb Cather* was different. On the cover was a picture of Zeb, their own sheriff, the man who had first brought Darby to this town of Running Springs.

Though she was not a good reader, Dolly had devoured the entire book again and again. Sometimes she liked to read it while Darby was nearby; she would look from the book to its author, and a great feeling of pride would well up inside her to know she loved such a man.

Did he love her? She thought so. But, except when an-
gered, he was not an expressive man. Primarily, he was
dedicated to the idea of capturing the West on the written
page, just the way it was, without sensation or exaggeration.
He had spoken to her many times of this; it was almost as if
he wished to atone for his earlier years of romanticized, dime-
novel writing. To succeed, he would have to travel into danger, in search of truth, in search of legends. Because he was a
stranger to the West and unfamiliar to its ways, Dolly
worried. But she understood how he felt and, therefore, was
willing to accept this. In a strange way, it suited her, for she
had never been attracted to men who were settled and permanent.

She owned the Antelope Hotel and, though it afforded her
a measure of security, it was also her prison. So, if Darby
Buckingham wanted to travel in search of adventure to write
about, that was fine with her, for she would be part of it—as
long as he returned each time to write and to love her.

She looked up, momentarily distracted. "You sure you
don't want to come and celebrate with us?" Zack Woolsey
said, poking his head through the door. "We'll be leavin'
directly."

"Not soon enough!"

Bear Timberly lumbered into the room, an almost empty
whiskey bottle clutched in one massive fist. He was still
barefoot and his hair was wet; Dolly could detect the strong
scent of soap. Somehow, she supposed, they had finally managed to get a bath without drowning each other.

"Sorry about his head," Bear said, "sorry as hell. Gonna
have a real knot there for sure."

He *was* sorry; Dolly could see that he honestly meant it. In
a way, she thought, they are like children—destructive, but
not for the sake of being destructive.

"Why don't you two gather up your supplies and leave
town?" she asked quietly. "You've had your bath, and

enough whiskey for a platoon of U.S. cavalry. You've had a good time, haven't you?"

"Well, yeah, but—"

"Yeah but nothing," she said, an edge of steel creeping into her voice. "You've been here less than two hours and already you've wrecked the John C. Fremont Suite and almost busted Darby's head. Now, I'll forgive you, but I don't think *he* will. When Darby wakes up, he's going to be very mad."

"Try to save him from hisself, then," Zack advised solemnly. "We'll be howling now; if you change your mind, we won't be hard to find."

"I can believe that," Dolly replied.

Bear Timberly sat on the floor, working his foot into his high-topped leather mocassins. When he had laced both, he stood up unsteadily. "Zack, maybe we should just get out now. Could be, the lady was right. Besides, now that I drowned the lice offa me, there ain't much else I want to do here."

Zack Woolsey shifted his weight, took a long pull from the bottle, and grinned across the room. "We have just seven hundred dollars," he said, suddenly growing thoughtful. "That's no fortune—not a lot to show for more'n thirty years of trapping."

Bear nodded. "What's on your mind?"

"Well, I just been wonderin' what we're going to do with ourselves. It seems to me like we ain't got quite enough money to set us up with the kinda ranch we been talking about all these years."

"Spit it out, Zack. I know you well enough to see you got an idea."

"Well, I could go down and play some cards." He saw the protest in Bear's eyes. "Now, look here, you know I'm good. Besides," he groused, "I feel lucky."

"I don't know," Bear said. "Hate to lose what we have."

"Yeah, me too," Zack added solemnly. "But it just seems to me like our whole lives have been a gamble. We got one more hand to play down there. If I can win, we buy ourselves some land. We both agreed we don't want to go North again. Ain't that so?"

"Yeah. Yeah, we did. But what if you lose?"

"Well," Zack said, "have try to make it one more winter in Canada, I guess."

"You better, by gawd, win, Zack. I don't want to go back up there!"

"Don't worry," Zack replied, feeling suddenly nervous. He took a hard drink and shoved off toward the door. "Besides, like I said, I feel lucky."

Edward Hyder leaned wearily back in his chair and surveyed the dusky interior of the Concord Saloon. It looked just like a thousand others he'd seen and it brought a touch of bitterness to his mouth. At fifty-three, with silver-shot brown hair, he was beginning to realize that success had passed him by. This awareness had added hard lines to a face that had once been lean and hawkishly handsome. But now, as he sat slumped at the table, he was conscious of the way his shirt bulged from too many years of soft living and hard drinking. But it hadn't been a bad life—it was just that he was tired of drifting, of lonely hotel rooms, and, yes, even of gambling.

Edward Hyder was enjoying his own mood of self-pity. He watched through heavy-lidded, bloodshot eyes as, across the street, a woman with a lunch basket paused to enter the gunsmith shop. The gambler had been in town more than three weeks and, by now, had the pulse beat of Running Springs at his fingertips. That was Mrs. Tiggert, the wife of Henry Tiggert, gunsmith, shop owner, respected citizen. The woman was about to enter when she was stopped by a well-dressed man in a familiar gray cloth suit. The banker looked like every banker he'd ever seen—pumped up with his own importance and immaculately groomed, not a hair out of place.

Hyder detested bankers. The man drew out a big gold watch and Hyder almost laughed. Every time he saw the man, he was dragging out that clock-sized watch. It was a habit the banker must have thought was impressive, as though he, of all people in town, was the only one who valued time. Hyder sneered; he'd love to steal that gawddamn watch. He'd tear the insides out of it and fill it with fresh green horse manure. A low giggle escaped from his mouth as he visualized the look on the banker's face when he pulled it out in front of someone. Yeah, that would really be something!

He continued to stare resentfully until they both laughed and the banker marched on while Mrs. Tiggert entered the shop. She was bringing her husband lunch. It was a daily ritual, but all at once it took on special meaning for the gambler. For no one had ever cared if he ate or went hungry. Sure, just a lunch—but somehow much more. Hyder knew loneliness.

In the beginning, gambling had been all he'd ever cared about. And he'd been given the necessary skills—long, supple fingers, with fingertips as sensitive to touch as the tongue of a snake, a keen ability to judge the skill of his opponents, and almost a sixth sense of when to close in for the kill.

Early in his career, he'd been wounded by a drunken loser; it was then he'd seen the value of being adept with a gun or knife. He still practiced when he was traveling the road between towns. There was one more advantage for the rare times he'd found himself overmatched or, more and more, when the luck of the cards fell against him: he could cheat.

As far as he was concerned, everyone cheated and a man who couldn't just hadn't learned the game. Besides, the only way to know if you yourself were being cheated was to be more deceptive than your opponent. It was simple.

Hyder unconsciously shuffled the deck in his hand. Yes, he

thought, staring across the street, perhaps I should have been a family man, a storekeeper, raising kids and having friends. A fella got tired of living alone, knowing no one cared whether he won or lost, lived or died. Once, there had been a girl. He shook his head a little sadly; what was the sense in going over the past? Still, perhaps it wasn't too late. Maybe this was the time. The place.

Mentally, he ran over his personal assets. He still had eleven hundred dollars left from a big-stakes game in Cheyenne. He laughed to himself. It would be a long while before he ever saw that town again. Damn wonder he'd gotten out alive. How much, he pondered, would it take to buy a place of his own? To buy respectability, and a good, respectable wife?

As far as he was concerned, everything was for sale. He'd seen nothing in his life to show him otherwise. People with influence were the ones who could afford it. It didn't matter what the man was inside; as long as he dressed the outside with fine clothes, he was a man to be respected. It had never seemed right to Hyder, but he'd watched people too long to believe otherwise. It just took money.

A fly droned overhead in a loose circle, almost as bored as he was. Across the room, Carl, the bartender, looked half asleep. There were only a half dozen men standing hipshot, absently drinking their beers. He knew they weren't interested in a game. They counted their change as if they were selling their fingers—one by one.

Gawd, he thought, looking down at the deck in his hands. There's got to be a better way. His forefingers brushed over the corners of the cards; unconsciously, he felt the tiny indentations on their surface and counted them off in his mind. He had a gifted set of fingertips; they'd never failed to earn his living. He saw Mrs. Tiggert emerge from the shop and watched as she kissed her husband and hurried off to do whatever women did. It would be kind of nice, he thought, if I had just a few more dollars.

Suddenly there was a loud, raucous laughing outside and the heavy sound of footsteps coming up the walk. A mask dropped over Hyder's face as the doors exploded in and two of the biggest, roughest-looking old men he'd ever seen rolled toward the bar. His practiced eye told him at a glance they were nearly drunk.

"Set 'em up!" the shorter one bellowed, slamming saddlebags on the bar for emphasis.

The men positioned at the bar turned irritably at the intrusion. They met two pair of hard, red-rimmed eyes, and their own glances returned to their beers.

"Whiskey. Your best!" Zack ordered.

The bartender was wide awake now. He spun around and produced a bottle. Hyder noticed that he did not let go of it, though. The bartender's voice carried to him. "You have cash, strangers?"

For a moment, Hyder figured the bartender had gone too far. The tall hunter in the coonskin hat stiffened, started to raise his rifle. But the shorter, more powerful-looking one saved the bartender from certain destruction. "Take it easy, Zack; he's just trying' to make a livin', like us. We already caused enough trouble, and stretchin' his ears wouldn't bring no satisfaction."

Zack relaxed visibly, then reached into his saddlebags and pulled out a thick packet of greenbacks. All at once, Hyder's pulse began to sprint. He watched the two men each take a drink, and then he finished his own and sauntered over to the bar, hoping he looked bored.

"How's it going, Carl?"

Carl only nodded.

"Damn slow around here today, ain't it?"

Carl's face clouded. Hyder knew the bartender didn't like

him and wouldn't play to his setup. "Got a feelin' it ain't going to stay that way," he grunted.

What a contrary sonofabitch! Hyder fumed. Roughly, he curbed his anger. "I was kind of hoping to get a game up. But," he shrugged, "I guess there ain't anybody with money in this town. A man gets damn tired of playing for chicken feed. Doesn't seem like there's many men left any more who are willing to gamble for real stakes."

A few feet away, Bear's hand clamped down on Zack Woolsey's arm. The gambler noticed it but showed nothing. This was a dangerous part. He brushed his sleeve against the bar top, and the small derringer gave him temporary assurance. A man with a purpose, he pressed the bait even harder. Normally, he set them up subtly. By the looks of these two, though, subtlety would be a waste.

"Remember, Carl," he said, as if he'd known the man for years, "how it was in the old days? Hell," he sneered, "back then a man would go for broke. They was really something."

The bartender was staring at him like he was crazy. It made Hyder nervous. "Well, don't just stand there, man; how about another beer! To the old days," he toasted, "when men weren't afraid to try their luck and the devil take tomorrow!"

"To the old days," Zack said quietly. "I'll join you in that. How 'bout it, Bear, the toast suit you?"

"Zack, he's setting you up."

"That's what he thinks."

Hyder grinned innocently. They weren't fooled and he knew it. He'd seen their type before. The last of the wild ones. And they always had to prove it. Taunt 'em a little, they'd play to your hand like children. Taunt 'em too much—they'd kill you.

"You looking for a game?" Zack asked.

Hyder nodded slowly, with his glass in his hand. "Always," he said smiling. "What kind of cards do you play?"

"Anything, long as it's worth my time."

"Well, sir, maybe you and I ought to move over to that table."

Zack shrugged. "Maybe we ought."

Darby Buckingham woke slowly, fighting pain and consciousness with every fiber of his being. He became aware of Dolly's presence and he wished she would go away and leave him in his agony. There was a building pressure inside his head, and, with his eyes screwed tightly shut, he tried to recall what had reduced him to this wretched state. Out of a swirling, crimson cloud, the leering faces of Bear Timberly and Zack Woolsey emerged. His anger flared, and the flame of it burned off the mist, and he opened his eyes to stare at Dolly. "Where are they?" he demanded, trying to rise.

"Oh, darling! Thank heavens you're awake! I'm so sorry I asked you to go over there!" she cried. "Will you ever forgive me?"

A tear fell wetly to crown off the enormous lump on his forehead. "Ouch!" he grunted. "For God's sake, Dolly, don't drip on me! Get my handkerchief and wipe your eyes." He stopped then; the misery on Dolly's face made him suddenly ashamed of his outburst. "Look," he tried, "I'm sorry I yelled at you. Besides, it wasn't your fault that I . . . I lost."

"But you didn't lose!" she protested, dabbing at her eyes. "The tall one said he had to hit you on the head with a bottle. He cheated!"

Darby had to grin at her answer. The question of fairness in winning or losing was one he knew Dolly wouldn't understand. A man who was winning, as he had been until he got himself beaned, could afford to fight fair. But to the man who was getting his brains beat in, fighting fair was the least of his concerns. Thinking back on it, he knew Zack had done the only thing he could have to save himself.

He managed to sit up. "Did they go back to their room?"

She hesitated.

"Dolly, I've got to find them, for their good as well as for the town's. Are you forgetting that I had to take over as sheriff while Zeb Cather is recovering?"

"No, but . . . but I'm afraid for you. What if they drew a knife, or a gun?"

"If they were killers, they would have finished me off next door. No," he said, "they're proud, and half drunk, and certainly more than a little crazy, but they're not killers. I'm sure of it. Still, they've destroyed your property and they'll have to pay or go to jail. I can't allow it to be otherwise. The thing to do now is to stop them, before they get drunk enough to try and demolish the whole town. Now, please, Dolly, where are they?"

"You should know," she said slowly, "that they said they were sorry for knocking you out with the bottle. They meant it too! I could tell by the way they said so."

"I'll remember that when I find them," he said, touching the knot on his forehead. "Now I better get going." He stood up, and felt dizzy. Taking a deep breath, he carefully walked across the room and changed into a stiff, white shirt. With his back to Dolly, he found that his fingers seemed numb and unresponsive as he fumbled to button it up. Maybe he'd been hit even harder than he'd first thought. Some fresh air, he decided, and I'll be fine.

"Dolly, get me coat out of the closet, please."

He pinned the sheriff's badge to his shirt and walked to his bureau. In the deep top drawer were three round, black felt derby hats. He selected the one he cared least about and cocked it low, almost to his eyebrows, so it covered the lump. Wordlessly, he lifted his arms as she helped him into the coat. There, he thought, studying himself in the mirror, I look nearly alive again. Without turning, his eyes fell down to the drawer. A silver-handled derringer lay waiting. Tentatively, he began to reach for it, then stopped. He pushed the drawer shut and turned. "How much do you think they owe you for damages?"

"Darby, I don't care—"

"How much?"

"Oh, ten dollars! But they said they'd pay!"

"Well, they were right about that much," he said, starting for the door.

"Darby?"

"Yes," he answered standing in the doorway.

"I don't want the damned money. I want you."

He winked painfully, and as he closed the door softly behind him, there was a smile on his face.

When he stepped out onto the boardwalk, however, the smile was gone. The descent of the stairs had impressed upon him how unfit he was to face any kind of trouble. His knees felt like cotton balls, loose and without strength. Standing outside now, he was surprised to see that the day's light was gone and the stores were closed. Except for the Concord Saloon, and farther down, the Bull Dog and Bent Bucket bars, Running Springs was locked up for the night. Dolly hadn't gotten around to telling him where Timberly and Woolsey had gone, but it really didn't matter. In a town this size, with only three bars, he could find them in less than ten minutes. He withdrew a long, rich-smelling Cuban cigar from his coat pocket, a match flared, and he inhaled deeply as his eyes covered the street.

In front of the two smaller bars, three horses stood hitched to the rails. Both places were quiet and Darby knew he would find only a few regulars and businessmen inside having a drink before going home. But, in the other direction, the Concord held promise of greater activity. It catered to a different breed. There were gambling tables and a piano; the piano, he thought, listening, had probably never been tuned. Darby figured that was where those two old fellas would go like buffalo to a mud wallow.

He remained where he was, smoking and thinking, taking his time, as he should have done before he'd burst into their room and paid the price for rushing. In the lamplight of the Antelope Hotel, his badge gleamed brightly. What am I, of all people, doing this for? Zeb Cather, of course.

But he was completely unqualified to try to fill Cather's boots and he knew it. Once again, he thought about how he couldn't even shoot straight; a fact the whole town found amusing. Yet, he was aware that they respected him too. He was an Easterner, and he dressed differently, but he'd once saved Zeb Cather's life and he'd written a book about the man. Apparently that made him sort of an honorary citizen in this town, an honorary sheriff. And he knew if he faced big trouble the citizens would stand behind him all the way.

His mind drifted back to New York City. It would be late there, but on the streets there'd still be a lively, party-going crowd. Yes, he sighed, he missed the big town, and yet . . . yet he was not eager to go back. Funny, he thought, after all those years with the circus, lifting weights, and then fighting for a crown . . . his mind skipped on. After all those years, he'd finally hit success—as a writer. A cynical expression formed on his lips. Writing dime novels had brought him a small measure of fame, and a large bank account, but not much else. Not, that is, until he had decided to go West and find the truth, document the great changes and men that were actually transforming the frontier into a Union.

The story of Zeb Cather was the best he'd ever done. And even though it had nearly cost him his life, it had been worth it. J. Franklin Warner, president of the New York Publishing House, had, at first, been dead set against his coming out here to write. But things had certainly changed: four days ago he'd sent a wire saying that the Cather book had topped anything he'd yet produced. It gave Darby a good feeling, and it convinced him he'd been right all along. Now, as he stood smoking the cigar, he felt restless to travel in search of other stories. But until Zeb Cather healed, he knew he had to stay. Besides, there was Dolly to consider. When the time came to leave, he knew he'd miss her the minute he was out of town.

The night was cool and a fresh breeze came off the snow-clad Tetons. Though there wasn't a full moon, their snowy pinnacles gleamed almost phosphorescently white. His eyes came back to the Concord as a loud shout escaped through the swinging doors. He should go, but yet he lingered. He wasn't afraid; still, he had to admit that facing those two again wasn't his idea of a good time. He decided he was hoping they'd leave so he could stop them on the street. Alone, they might be peacefully talked into paying for their damages and leaving. In front of others, their pride would force them to fight.

Darby Buckingham curled his fingers into a fist. Good, he breathed, the numbness was gone, and his grip felt strong. He studied his cigar; five more minutes, he decided, then I'm going to have to go down to the Concord and face up to them. He took a deep pull on the cigar, which made it glow brightly red against his badge. Thunder and lightning! I'll be glad when Zeb's wearing this, Darby thought angrily. It was time to move.

CHAPTER 5

Zack Woolsey shifted uncomfortably in his chair. His mouth was set in a hard, bitter line and his eyes were bright and bloodshot. They had been playing for just over three hours. He scrubbed his face with a rough, callused hand and glared across the table at Edward Hyder. He hated the man. Hated the cool, passionless way he played and the steadily mounting pile of greenbacks that reminded Zack he had been losing all along. An hour ago, he'd lost all of his own money; now he was even losing Bear's.

Zack's gaze fell to the pitiful stack that remained. Angry shame was in his stomach and, for the last hour, he hadn't even been able to meet Bear's eyes. He didn't want to see the misery that he knew he'd find, but there was something that Bear didn't know: Hyder was a cheat. The problem was Zack couldn't, for the life of him, figure out *how* Hyder was cheating; he was completely stumped. It had happened time and time again: the gambler had bet with a sense of certainty that went far beyond skill. Some way, the man had the game rigged. But how? Zack raged, how could he know my hand? It wasn't any way that Zack had ever seen before. He was sure of only that much. He'd stared until his eyes ached. The gambler wasn't palming, dealing from the bottom, or keeping hide-away cards. These tricks would have been spotted hours ago, no matter how good Hyder was. Jeezus, Zack groaned wearily, I better figger him out quick, or it's back to Canada for sure.

As Hyder dealt, Zack received his cards almost with

indifference. He no longer cared about winning the hand—all he wanted was to expose this man who took his money with a casual air of certainty. If Zack could catch him at his game, it would be a simple matter of justice to take back everything he'd lost—even if he had to kill Hyder. Dead or alive, it didn't much matter as far as Zack was concerned, the gambler was no better than a scorpion, and Wyoming would be better off with him under sod. Zack focused on his cards and tried to guess what Hyder would do. The man knew what he held, as damnedly sure as if they had been dealt face up on the table before him. Sometimes, Zack remembered, Hyder would let him win when the stakes were small. But now he held three sixes and the gambler was no doubt counting on pushing the bet up and taking him big.

Zack peeked up from his cards and studied Hyder. The face was expressionless and, if he was nervous, it didn't show. Yet Zack could feel the man's tension clear through the table. Most gamblers, he knew, would have taken more time to win than this one. Hyder was a very greedy cheat and it was going to be his downfall—he hoped. Zack raised the man and took another pull from his bottle. "Call," he spat.

The hand, as he'd guessed, was played and Hyder won again. Zack gripped the table's edge, trying to keep his fury contained. He bored through the gambler with hot, deadly eyes. You son of a bitch! he thought, what the hell are you doing to me? If Bear had suspected what was going on, he would have acted characteristically—dismember the gambler. But Zack knew better. Even in a town this size, you couldn't get away with just shooting the winner and taking your money back. That kind of thing could get you hanged quick. If you called a man a cheat and killed him, you'd better be able to back up your claim with some proof. It was a hell of a deal, but it was universally understood that the outcome of a card game didn't simply rest on who was the fastest on the trigger. Those days, Zack thought sadly, are as gone as the buffalo herds. Grudgingly, Zack could see it made sense—but as far as this game went, he'd be happy to suspend the rules.

Zack dealt and won thirty dollars, which didn't surprise him at all. When he was dealing, he won as often as not. Early in the game, he'd decided that the gambler's edge lay in the way he passed out the cards. Thirty dollars was the biggest hand he'd won all afternoon. He's gettin' spooky, Zack told himself, and that's gonna make it harder.

He watched the gambler shuffle the cards; the man's long, white fingers were thin and womanish. It was an honest shuffle, as far as he could see—out away from his body and open.

"Cut."

Zack cut once, and leaned back in his chair. Several times, he'd cut the deck oddly, just to see, and it hadn't made a damn bit of difference. At least it narrowed the possibilities. Whatever the gambler was doing had to be on the deal.

Here he goes again, Zack thought, tensing, and his eyes bugged, he stared so hard. As for the cards he received, Woolsey didn't even look at them. He was aware of nothing but the long, moving fingers. Suddenly, Zack felt his stomach go tight! Either the man habitually rubbed the cards as they passed through those delicate fingers, or he had them marked in a way that escaped detection. Zack leaned forward then, crowding the table. The fingers paused for a moment and Zack saw the man's forefinger quiver. Then, just as quickly, it moved and the thumb brushed the back of his card and kicked it across the table.

"Deal me three more," he demanded.

The fingers caressed the cards again. Zack felt his heart skip—he knew. It *was* in the deal! But how, he wondered, can I prove it? He quickly studied the cards in his hand, tilting them first one way, then the other. There was a kerosene lamp hanging somewhere behind him, but the poor light it gave was made even worse by the shadow of his body. He could see nothing. "Get me a cigar," he mumbled to Bear.

Bear Timberly lurched unsteadily to his feet. He felt like hell. This had been one of the worst afternoons in his life. He couldn't understand what had gone wrong. All he knew was that their stake was almost wiped out. "Sure, why not?" Bear slurred caustically, "anything you say, partner!"

Zack avoided Bear's eyes. He knew what he was thinking and his partner had a right to feel as he did. Still, Zack knew he couldn't break away from the game in order to explain. Besides, Bear would get violent. Zack didn't want his friend to wind up in a noose. But at last, Zack thought, I'm onto his game. Behind him, he heard Bear trip over a chair and utter a low oath. He could hear him at the bar now, and knew Bear was ordering yet another bottle. A few minutes later, he returned with the cigar and matches. He threw them down on the table and stalked over to his chair, hunched down, and began to brood.

In an exaggerated show of lighting his cigar, Zack scraped a match and held it low. His eyes searched the cards and, under the intense light of the match—he found what he wanted. There were thin, almost invisible indentations each cupped enough to tell him they were the imprint of Hyder's thumbnail. Zack ran his fingers over them. He felt nothing. But under the match's glare, he counted them slowly along the backs of the face cards. He finished lighting his cigar, then slowly reached out to take the deck. Hyder's grip, when it struck, was surprisingly strong on his wrist. With a low, hissing voice, he said, "What the hell are you doing!"

"You're a cheat, mister, and I'm going to prove it, right now!"

Hyder's face went as white as his hand. "Gawddamn you!" he choked. "You're a lying bastard who—"

Zack jumped out of his chair and swung with his free hand.

His fist drove level across the table and his knuckles flattened Hyder's nose into a bloody pulp as the man careened over backward in his chair. Zack started around the table. His hands were outstretched and eager to throttle the cheat to death. In midstride he saw, too late, the gun in Hyder's fist. With a bellow, he twisted and the sharp bark of a high-caliber weapon snapped across the Concord as Zack Woolsey felt a hammer blow smash into his skull. He staggered; his legs went to wood. There was a thick, acrid cloud of gunsmoke between him and Hyder, and he tried to claw through it. He couldn't. Everything was whirling and he heard a boot slam down close; then Hyder was there and hacked him with his gun belt. Zack Woolsey fell like a rock in a deep, muddy river. At the last moment, he thought he heard a second shot and a shout from Bear. Then he heard nothing.

At the sound of the first shot, Darby Buckingham was yanked out of his reverie. He spat the Cuban cigar out of his mouth with an oath and whirled just as the second gunshot split the night air. He knew without even thinking what had happened. The goddamn drunken buffalo hunters had killed someone. He began to run.

Darby was rock solid, a block of granite, an indomitable force. But he was not a runner. In fact, he really didn't know how to run. To his mind, it was beneath his dignity. But someone had just been shot and it was his own fault for standing around smoking a cigar.

It was only sixty yards to the Concord Saloon, but it seemed like sixty miles. His short, muscled legs simply refused to move with any speed. Every stride was a pounding agony as the derby he wore nudged the newly formed goose egg on his forehead. His brain seemed to slap the interior of his cranium with demented intent. Darby tried to yank his gun out of the holster, but it got caught in the inside lining of his coat and refused to come loose.

He shuddered to a halt. "Damn you!" he swore, tearing the gun free and hearing the lining rip. He pushed the gun out before him, took a deep breath, and charged the bat-wing doors. He would not have been at all surprised to see the two old mountain men eye-balling him down the barrels of their great, long rifles.

Instead, he saw a gambler being choked to death. Bear Timberly had him bent half double over the bar. His powerful hands were locked on Hyder's throat and he was bearing down with terrible intensity. A low rattle told Darby that it would be over in a moment.

"Stop!" Bear didn't seem to hear him. "Stop or I'll shoot you!" Still no response. Darby held the gun up to fire. He sighted at the broad expanse of leather between the shoulder blades. Darby grimaced. Who was he kidding? He wasn't going to shoot, and even Bear must have known it. "Damn," he muttered, holstering his weapon with disgust.

He hooked an arm around Bear's neck and pulled. The man took a back step, then surged forward to renew his assault. Reluctantly, Darby let go and stepped back. There was no choice. He yanked his gun out and, shaking his head sadly, he cracked Bear across the back of his skull. There was a grunt. A sagging of muscles, then nothing. He didn't even shake his head! Darby struck again, harder. Very hard, in fact. Bear groaned, slumped, and fell.

For a moment, the only sound in the room was the whooping gasps of Hyder. The man had very nearly been finished. Darby saw his eyes. They were wild, unfocused, protruding. Hyder seemed unable to move. He was half propped up against the bar, his feet widely spread, his body rigid except for the heaving chest. His neck seemed bent back at some queer angle and his mouth was shaped in a silent, gasping scream. Darby had to look away.

Across the room he located the taller hunter. Darby saw him sprawled on the floor, his face sheeted with blood. He rushed over and felt the man's pulse. It was steady. When he knelt closer, he saw that Zack had suffered only a flesh wound. Nasty-looking but superficial. Probably, it had just momentarily stunned him.

He found a derringer. Both barrels empty and near by. Nobody had to tell him it was the gambler's. He'd bet anything there'd been a card game and the two strangers had drawn the short end of the hand. Buffalo rifles were no match with a derringer at close range.

Money and cards soaked with whiskey and blood. That was what Darby saw scattered about the back part of the Concord. Suddenly a cry exploded: "Oh, no! No!"

Bear was back on the gambler. Same position, same objective. He was so huge his body totally blocked out the gambler. All Darby could see was a thin pair of flailing legs. The smaller man was completely off his feet. The heels of his boots beat frantically against the bar.

In an instant, Darby knew there was no hope of reaching them in time. So he did the only thing he could think of. He pulled his gun and aimed it at Bear's head and fired. He missed, just as he knew he would. But not by much. Bear must have heard the bullet's whine, because he whirled around and Darby had him square in his sights.

"This time I go for the body," he said. "And I can't miss." Hyder slumped to the floor holding his throat. Neither man noticed, and Darby wondered if the gambler was finished. "Did you kill him?"

The question seemed to throw Bear off balance. He frowned, then glanced down at his victim. "He can still move and squeak so I guess not."

"My neck. He broke my neck!" It was a cry, but unlike anything that would come out of a normal human being. Not a voice, really; more like a tortuous wheeze.

Bear stepped over the man and hurried to his friend. "If he's dead—"

"He isn't," Darby said, moving to Hyder. He knelt close to the man. "As soon as you recover, I'll want a statement."

"Whiskey!" the gambler croaked.

Darby nodded to the bartender. The drink put some strength into Hyder. "I won from the tall one. He went crazy . . . just all of a sudden. Busted me in the nose. I fired. Then the other almost strangled me!" He swallowed noisily. "Good God, did you see him?"

"I saw."

"He was cheating!" Bear yelled. "Zack said he was!"

"How would you know?" Darby countered. "You and your friend were half drunk when you jumped me." He gritted his teeth in fury. "If that's the best you've got, I'll have to arrest you. Maybe a few days in jail and we'll find out the truth. Although I think I already know what that will be."

"Shit, mister. You wouldn't know the truth if it walked up and kicked you!"

"You two old men are so uncivilized you'd put a savage to shame! Know that?" Darby roared.

Bear ignored him.

"Carl, bring this man some more whiskey and a towel to clean this mess off his face."

"Yessir."

"What happened? You must have seen it all. Those two claim they were cheated. Any truth to it?"

Carl ran his hands nervously down his shirt front. "I wish I could say, Mr. Buckingham. Truth of the matter is that I was keeping as far away from back there as I could. It was clear what was going to happen."

"In what way?"

"Well, like you said. They were half loaded and primed for trouble." For a moment, the bartender's eyes fell on Hyder. "I don't much care for professionals to come in my place, but as long as they pay for their drinks and don't antagonize my customers, I can't ask 'em to leave. And believe me, Darby, this man just opened fire trying to save his life. First the taller one yelled and called him a cheat, then they were both after him."

"That settles it," Darby said. "You and your friend are under arrest."

"No jail," Bear said slowly. "We won't be penned in a jail. Have to kill us first."

Confound it, Darby thought. What in the world am I going to do now? He stood there for a moment feeling half sick and half defeated. I wonder if Zeb Cather ever found himself in a mess like this. It was a wreched dilemma if ever there was one.

Hyder saved him. "I'd have to press charges against them, wouldn't I?"

"Yes, but—"

"I won't do it. No way! Sheriff, I want them run out of town."

"Why?"

"Huh?"

"Why don't you want to press charges?" Darby asked.

Hyder placed the towel on the bar. "Give me a whiskey, Carl." He turned back to Darby. "You don't like me, do you?"

"No."

"Thank you for your honesty, at least. Now I'll level with you, Mr. Buckingham. I'm a professional. And a professional always calculates the odds." He absently dropped a dollar on the bar, then held his whiskey up in mock salute. "My calculations are that you ain't sheriff enough to hold those two in jail. To be frank, I'd feel a hell of a lot safer if they were run out of town."

"How much did you take them for?"

The answer was slow in coming. The gambler swallowed his whiskey in a gulp. Nodded for another. "I don't see that it's any of your business."

Darby smiled. "Bear, you want to finish what you started?"

The man's eyes were close. They widened with fear. "You wouldn't! You're the sheriff!"

"He's all yours, Bear."

"Wait! I took 'em for about six hundred. Maybe six-fifty."

"Fast work," Darby said dryly. "You must be pretty good."

"It's my business to be."

"I'm sure it is." Darby glanced over at the hunters. "You said your friend was cheated. How?"

Bear shrugged. "Don't know. But if Zack says he was cheated, he was cheated."

"I need proof."

"Not me. One way or another, we'll get even. That's . . . that's our money."

He didn't understand whether Bear was too drunk to reason or whether he was incapable of accepting that the times had changed; justice was based on hard evidence. All Darby was sure of was that, without proof, there was no way to handle these two except to run them out of town. "You and your friend are leaving Running Springs. Now."

For a second, Darby thought that Bear was going to jump for him. But he didn't. He just said, "We shoulda throwed you out the window when we had you down. We went soft and that was our mistake. Won't make it again, city man. Be remembering that."

"I will."

Without another word, Bear pulled one of Zack's arms across his round shoulders and half-carried, half-dragged the man out the door. Darby walked over to the overturned table. Money and cards and an empty whiskey bottle lay in scattered profusion. "How much of this money belongs to them, Hyder?"

"Fifty dollars at most," the man said, stepping over. "The rest is mine!"

Darby squatted and gathered up a hundred dollars even. He started to rise, hesitated, and picked up an ace of hearts and a four of diamonds. He studied them for a moment in silence. He couldn't see any irregularity at all. But, then, he hadn't expected to. Still, as he knelt there, Darby searched for some clue. It was possible that Hyder was telling the truth. The hunters were reckless, unprincipled men and both had been drinking heavily. Perhaps Zack Woolsey was inept at poker. It was likely the same scenario had been repeated in a dozen frontier towns. Maybe. But he doubted it.

"I said only fifty is their's. The rest is mine."

Darby dropped the cards soundlessly. He stood erect, his eyes level with those of Edward Hyder. "Your nose is bent. You better collect your winnings and go see the doctor." Before the man could reply, he walked away. He stopped for a moment and gathered the two buffalo rifles on his way out.

On the boardwalk, he waited while Bear got the horses and started up the street toward him. In the moonlight he had no trouble at all making them out. Bear rode in front, thick, hunched deeply in his saddle. He'd tied a lead rope to Zack's horse. Behind him, the lean man sat bent, rocking to the motion of his mount. They pulled up before the Concord. "I'll be taking our rifles."

Darby stepped into the street and handed the weapons up. He walked around to Zack. "You going to be all right? Maybe you should see our doctor. You could leave tomorrow."

"No," came a heavy reply. "I can ride. I can make it." His breathing was fast. "Until we return, sheriff."

"If you return, someone is going to die."

Somehow, Zack straightened in his saddle, pushed himself up against his saddle horn. Darby watched him weave slightly, saw the black sheet of dried blood that covered the near side of his face. "Nobody lives forever . . . nobody. And . . . and that gambler's time is come. Yours, too, if you interfere."

"That isn't the way. Can't you two understand that it doesn't work like that any more? Proof, man! Give me proof and I'll arrest him."

"Come on, Zack!" Bear reined his horse away. The lead rope pulled Zack's horse around so abruptly the taller man was almost unseated. Deep anger flashed inside Darby. He pivoted and grabbed the rope. With a vicious yank, he pulled Bear half out of his saddle. "Enough!" he shouted.

He was aware that he was out of control. A sheriff wasn't supposed to stand in the street yelling. Zeb Cather wouldn't lose control. The hell with it; he wasn't Zeb Cather. He was a man who had been pushed to the limit. "Get out of that saddle," he yelled, raising his fists. "I'm going to pound sense into your skull."

Bear started to unload.

"No!" Zack croaked. "Not now. Leave him be. He just thinks he's doing his job."

"Trying to!" Darby exploded. He moved close to Zack, looked up into the pain-ridden face. "If it's any help, I believe you. But I still need proof."

Zack laughed, but it wasn't the kind of laugh that would cause a man to smile. "Proof! Proof, you say? Mister, gettin' proof cost me and Bear a winter's wages." He leaned out toward Darby, his face hideous and wild. "The proof is those marked cards he used."

"I examined one of the aces. I detected nothing."

"Of course you didn't," Zack stormed. "What did you expect? Notches on the edges?"

"No, but. . . ."

"They're scratched with his thumbnail, I'd guess. Had me fooled too—until the end." He shook his head. "He's slick, I'll give that to him. And if you notice, he plays at the back table, where the light ain't so good. I had to light a match to see the marks. Somehow, the bastard has enough touch to count 'em without even looking. Look at my hands, city man."

Darby stared at Zack's hand. "Your point, sir?"

"My hands are all hide and scar and warts. But that gambler probably never lifted anything heavier than a whiskey bottle. He's got fingers like a whore. Soft, womanish, and white." Zack leaned over and spit into the street. "Someday I'm goin' to cut them hands of his off at the wrists!"

Darby wiped his forehead, feeling sweat pop. "You don't have to do that. Let's go back inside and have a look at those cards. Show me the marks and I'll throw Hyder in jail and return your money."

"How long we been outa there?"

"Five, maybe ten minutes. Why?"

"How long do you figure it would take that snake to gather up those cards and switch decks?" He gave Darby one last, contemptuous look. "Throw me the lead rope, Bear. And let's get outa here. It smells bad."

Darby growled and shoved one hundred dollars at the man, then stepped away.

"What's this for?"

"It's yours."

Zack simply nodded, then gigged his horse forward after his friend. Twenty yards down the street he reined in, then turned and called back. "We'll be back, Mr. Derby Man. This goddamn town ain't seen the last of us. Not by a long shot. Do yourself a favor. Don't be here when we come!"

Darby watched them ride out. He was troubled and felt a sense of inexplicable failure. He'd handled it wrong. The two riders turned the corner by the livery and were gone. But for how long? he wondered. For how long?

CHAPTER 6

Darby hurried back toward the saloon as soon as the two riders were gone. At the bat-wing doors, he stopped and looked inside. Deep in shadow at the far end of the room, he saw the gambler sitting alone. Darby pushed his way inside. Out of the corner of his eye he saw Carl coming from behind the bar with a bucket and mop.

"Want to get the blood up before it stains," he mumbled.

"Hyder," Darby said, "I see you didn't waste any time picking up your money and the cards."

The man glanced up at him with a peculiar, sideways twist of his upper body. "My money, my cards," he answered. "Why do you ask?"

"No reason." Darby decided to switch the subject. Zack had been right. If the cards were marked, it was too late now to find out. Maybe, he thought, if I keep quiet, I can catch him myself. The thing to do, though, is to pretend ignorance. "How's your neck?"

"It's killing me," came the gritted reply. "I had Carl send for the doctor. You shouldn't have let him jump me that second time. Right deep inside my brain I heard my neck pop. That's when it went. You shouldn't have let that happen. It was your job to kill him rather than let him do it to me that way."

"Sure. I'll remember that next time."

Hyder's eyes closed to slits. "I'd say something, Sheriff, but it'd only make you mad and I'm not looking for an argument. But it ain't going to happen 'next time.' Not to me, anyway.

I'm leaving this town on the first stage. You see . . . somehow I don't trust you. Call it a gambler's instinct, but I have a hunch you half believed that crazy man. Took his word over mine."

"That's not true. I'm sworn to uphold the rights and to protect the lives and property of the *respectable* citizens of Running Springs. And you're a *respectable* citizen, aren't you?"

The eyes closed again. "You're trying to bait me, Mr. Buckingham. It won't work. Besides, like I said, I'm leaving for healthier parts. Now, if you don't mind, please leave me alone. My throat hurts to talk."

"Of course," Darby said. "I'll go see if the doctor is on his way. You must be in great pain."

He almost collided with the doctor on the boardwalk. "Hold up a minute," he said, grabbing the man and pulling him back. "I want a few words with you first."

Protest rose in Dr. Sawyer's face. "But I've got a patient to see!"

"It's only his neck. And you're a specialist with bent necks, aren't you? Please, a word first."

"Well?"

"He mustn't travel, Doctor."

Dr. Sawyer wore very thick glasses. He blinked several times, quick, rabbit-like. "I don't see—"

"Tell him his neck is cracked, that's all."

"If his neck was even cracked a little he'd be paralyzed or dead, Mr. Buckingham!"

"He doesn't know that. Put a big cast around it. Tell him to travel could prove fatal. Tell him the bouncing of a horse or even the stagecoach would surely kill him."

"But why?"

Darby shifted around until he was between the man and the doorway. "Because it's sheriff's business and I need an excuse to keep him under observation. If you don't do as I ask, he will leave town and a very serious injustice will have been done."

"Oh, oh, I see," the doctor said, not seeing at all. "But you must remember I have the obligation of my oath."

"Of course! The Hippocratic oath. Let me assure you, Dr. Sawyer, I would not ask you to violate or compromise that noble pledge. But the man you are about to attend does have a serious neck injury."

"True, I'm sure. But—"

"Tell me, Doctor. Do you subscribe to a medical journal of some sort?"

"Of course," came an offended reply.

"Perhaps, if I am successful, I could write an article for that journal, describing how you played an important—and medically ethical, I will add—role in bringing a dangerous cardsharp to justice."

"You could do that?" The doctor's eyes widened. "Do you really think it would be published?"

"Which journal would you prefer?"

"*American Medicine?*" He said it in almost a whisper.

Darby pursed his lips thoughtfully. "*American Medicine.* Well. . . ."

The man seemed to deflate. "I should have known better than to ask. Even you couldn't swing that. It's the most prestigous medical journal in existence."

"Where is it published?"

"New York City."

Darby grinned. "In that case, I can almost guarantee our piece will see print. You see, I do have connections in New York. Extensive connections. My publisher, Mr. J. Franklin Warner most certainly knows the editor of *American Medicine* on a first-name basis."

The doctor's eyes were wide; his face assumed almost a dreamy quality. Darby nodded with satisfaction. He knew that frontier physicians were regarded by the eastern medical society as only slightly more advanced than voodoo men. Often, they had very little education, sometimes they were really horse doctors or dentists trying to serve the needs of an area where no certified doctor would practice. And even if they had attended medical school, they quickly became outdated on the frontier. He had no idea of the qualifications or background of the Running Springs practitioner. But he had correctly guessed Dr. Sawyer's need for professional recognition. "It will be published," he said quietly. "You have my word."

The doctor shook himself back to the present. His pale eyes fluttered behind thick lenses. "You want me to order him to stay bedridden?"

"No. In fact, I'd rather he continue his profession."

"I see. I see."

"I'd hoped you would. Just keep him in Running Springs. That's all that's required."

After the doctor went inside, Darby withdrew another cigar. Somehow, he would find out the truth. If the gambler was using marked cards, it was of the utmost urgency that he be arrested as quickly as possible. On the day that the two hunters returned, Darby wanted Hyder either out of town or in jail and their money returned. Anything else would lead to bloodshed.

"Yoo hoo! Darby, honey."

The cigar sagged in his mouth. Frowning, he glanced toward the upper floor of the Antelope Hotel. The look was unnecessary. He knew that voice very well. Darby puffed faster, tried to ignore her.

"When are you coming upstairs?"

Blast! he thought. He glanced up and down the street. No one in sight.

"Hurry up, honey, I'm lonesome."

Dolly's long, blond hair shone in the lamplight of her room. That was all he could see—just the face and that hair.

Like an angel. "I'll be right up, Miss Beavers," he said quietly. "Soon as I finish my evening cigar." Though he didn't move, he smoked fast.

Zack felt as though the top of his head was about to explode. Somehow, they had ridden until dawn. He was sick, humiliated, and full of hate for Running Springs. Every step of the way, Zack was punished. With the first light in the eastern sky, they had reached the south fork of the Shoshone River Crossing. He couldn't go any farther.

No words were spoken between the two men as they guided their horses down to the water and dismounted. He was shocked at how weak he felt. His legs seemed barely able to hold his weight. Zack squatted by the river and began to soak the dried blood from his face. Somewhere up the bank behind him, he heard the sounds of Bear getting sick. Too much whiskey. For both of them.

As the light grew stronger, he remained by the river. The water was cold, deep with spring runoff. Zack found himself unwilling to leave this place. Once, he twisted around and saw Bear curled up asleep. Zack knew he should do the same, but there was no sense in even trying. The sickness he felt wouldn't go away with rest. It was more than physical. Deep in thought, he contemplated the humiliation and injustice he had suffered in Running Springs. The blame was his, not Bear's. It had been himself who had lost their stake.

"Damn!" he raged at his reflection. "You're a fool. What has happened to your guts, Zack Woolsey? You should have shot that double-dealin' son of a bitch and considered it good riddance. You know he was cheatin'. That was always enough, before. But last night you went soft. Tried to get proof first. Damn you, Woolsey! You're an old, scared man!"

For the first time in years, he really looked at himself as he squatted in the mud and the sun climbed higher. What he saw that morning filled him with a profound sadness. He saw a beaten, haggard relic who had passed his prime somewhere and never realized it. At water's edge, the current was clear and he was shocked at how his eyes started back at him from deep hollows. "Too old," he whispered.

Zack guessed that humans were the only living animals that hung around past their natural time. The things he'd hunted all his life never grew old. No, from the first creaking of the bones, or the loss of teeth, deer, wolf, and even the mighty grizzly faced approaching death. An animal that could not graze because of bad teeth soon grew thin and weak. It either died by the fang, if it was lucky, or starved to death in a snowbank. With every animal, the results were the same. Only man fought the timetable of life—and tried to change it.

Absently, he reached down and scooped up a handful of sand. Still not changing his position, Zack squeezed the sand until it oozed between his long fingers and splashed into his reflection. Better, he thought. I should go quick. Die in a fight. Maybe my time was last night and somehow that eastern dude Buckingham had changed it.

"Zack?"

He started, the sand spilled from his grip. "Thought you were sleepin' it off."

"Why you hunched down over the water so long, Zack? You sick, like me?"

"Maybe."

"You're thinkin' about last night, aren't ya?"

Zack took a deep breath, let it out slow.

"Wasn't your fault, Zack. If you'd a won, you'd a shared the winnings. Like always. Nothing changed, Zack. Now we'll just share the loss. I don't much care."

"Sure you do, Bear. Don't try lying to me. You're as tired of scratchin' around this country as me. And you don't want to go North again, do you?"

"One more year, it'd make no difference."

"You had pneumonia, Bear. Remember? Almost killed you.

They tell me once a man's had it, he's likely to contract it again. No second chances." Zack snapped his fingers. "They die."

"Every man's got to do it sometime."

"That's what I was thinking, myself. Bear, you reckon I've lived too long?"

Before Zack could even move, Bear swung a foot that caught him square in the breeches and sent him flying into the river. When he hit the water, Zack's chest seemed to constrict. The current was swift and he broke water and struck out for shore, swearing with every gagging breath he took. He could see Bear running along the bank parallel with him. The man was hooting something Zack couldn't hear. He was waving his arms and, every time Zack's face cleared water for air, he could see that Bear was laughing.

Almost dead, Zack felt his hands claw the rocks a quarter mile from their camp. He felt Bear take a hold on his shirt and drag him up on the bank. The blood was surging in his head; he coughed up water. A chill shook his entire length.

Without a word, Bear lifted him off the ground, and Zack felt himself being thrown double over the man's shoulder. It was the most insulting position he'd ever been in in his entire life. He couldn't help it. He was exhausted, shaking, and sick. "Why?" he managed to gasp, staring at the bouncing ground before his eyes.

Bear didn't break stride as he answered. "You asked me if you'd lived too long. I decided you had to answer that one yourself."

"But I didn't say nothing!"

"Didn't need to, Zack. You swum out of it, didn't you? Seems to me that ought to be answer enough!"

They camped by the Shoshone River for two days. Eating fresh-caught fish, drinking gallons of water, and recovering from the whiskey. Twice, they saw the Concord stage thunder over the crossing downstream, almost a mile away. And each time, the two men would look at each other and know they were each thinking of where the stage was headed. Running Springs. The very thought of it was like a festering sore that would not heal.

Finally, it was Bear who came to grips with it.

"We going back soon?"

"Yep," Zack said.

"Want to saddle up now?"

"Tomorrow. Tomorrow we'll ride. But not back to that town until we've got more lead and powder. Running short, we are."

"Only takes one bullet to kill a snipe like that gambler. Could use our knives, even."

"I don't want to sneak in, Bear. I want to tail that town. I want to shoot the hell out of 'er. Understand?"

"What about the sheriff?"

"What about him?" Zack asked. "He's been warned. If the man has the sense of a prairie dog, he'll jump in a hole and stay covered. Funny, though, but I'd kinda hate to drill him."

"I'll do it. My bet is that he's probably in cahoots with the gambler. Wouldn't surprise me at all if they split our money between them."

"Nope. Nope, I don't think so. But just to make sure, I'll try and remember to ask the gamblin' man before he cashes in. Remind me of that, Bear, if you remember."

"Sure. But if we're not going to Running Springs, where are we going?"

"Snakegrass Junction. Less than a half day's ride on the other side of the river."

Bear chuckled softly. "Been so long I almost forgot about it. Hell, it's been four, maybe five years since we rode through. Wasn't much, I recollect."

"Well, don't worry. No doubt the place will be crawling with goddamn farmers. Let's ride."

The Shoshone River Crossing was a long, solid bridge spanning the river by five feet in the spring and as much as twelve feet in August, when the water level dropped to its lowest point.

Nobody knew who'd built it. Really, it was a collection of logs and lumber set on two massive piles in the center of the river. To look at it, a lone horseman would have felt his stomach tighten. In fact, when the water was down, most men preferred to swim their horses rather than use the bridge. It looked that bad. But, right now, the water was high and, besides, hadn't they both seen the stage pass across twice during their recovery?

"Look," Zack grunted as they approached. "Here comes the stage again."

"Be nice to get some chewing tobacca."

"Well, somebody's bound to have some spare."

"Them drivers got a schedule. He won't stop for us, Zack."

"He won't have no choice. Come on, let's wait for him on the bridge."

Their horses' hoofs sounded strange on the wood. Zack's mount shied back. He cut it a lick across the rump and the animal vaulted onto the crossing.

"God damn, Zack. I saw the bridge move."

"Come on! If the coach can make it, we sure as hell can." The sound of Bear's horse clattered woodenly behind him.

"He sees us, Zack. He ain't slowin' down."

"He will."

But he didn't. With growing apprehension, Zack saw the driver shift the reins to one hand and reach down toward his feet. When he straightened, there was a shotgun cradled in his arms. "Damn fool!" Zack swore.

With the recent humiliation of Running Springs still burning inside him, Zack was in no mood to give ground. As far as he was concerned, the bridge was as much his as anyone's, and he was on it first. "He's got to be bluffin'. I'll prove it."

He yanked his horse's head up close, dallied the reins around his saddle horn, and shouldered the buffalo rifle. He was a crack shot. Recognized as such even by his few remaining peers. It was his intent to send a ball through the crown of the driver's hat. Scare the hell out of him. But, try as he might, he couldn't set his sights. It was the horse that undermined his purpose. The damned animal began to buck in fear. Not great leaps with the idea of unseating its rider, but crazy, hopping bounces as if it wanted to relocate in any and every direction except facing the huge Concord stage and six charging horses. Suddenly, it happened. Zack felt the rear of his horse drop over the edge. The stage struck the far end of the bridge at a full run. Zack lost his balance. The horse seemed to hang on its stomach. A quick backward glance downward told Zack he did not want to go back into the boiling current. He dropped his rifle and leapt for the bridge. The stage thundered closer. "Shoot, Bear! Burn the bastard! What the. . . ."

Bear tried. But his own horse was out of control. The logs upon which it stood rattled. His animal reared and Zack saw with horror the rifle start to drop. But Bear caught it. Half in, half out of his saddle, the man made a desperate stab, and in doing so, he accidently pulled the trigger. Amid the thundering of the stage, Zack barely heard the weapon fire. He only saw the muzzle smoke blast downward. The entire underside of Bear's mount smelt of burnt horse hair. With a terrible bellow, the animal catapulted into the sky, and both man and beast dropped into the river with a hiss and a holler.

Before Zack saw them disappear, the lead horse in the stage team knocked him spinning. His last thought before hitting water was to hang onto his rifle. The last words he yelled were drowned in a gurgle.

Snakegrass Junction was dead. A ghost town. As the pair rode in from the west, the only thing they saw moving on the street was a tumbleweed. The sound of their horses' hoofs seemed very loud between the empty buildings. To Zack, it seemed hard to believe that a town could go to hell in such a hurry. But it had. Broken windows and doors, store signs face down in the dust. No people sounds, no people smells. An up-stairs graveyard is what it reminded him of. The buildings ran for only a hundred yards or so, and at the end the prairie was waiting. The whole thing was scary. Zack checked an impulse to set spurs and race through the wooden gauntlet and never look back. They were almost out when the man yelled.

"Hey! What are you doing in my town?"

Two rifles cocked in unison and came to rest on the apparition.

"Don't shoot! I'm unarmed."

"Who are you?" Zack called.

The man smiled gold teeth. He whipped off his bowler and bowed slightly. Though of medium size, he seemed to inflate. His voice was as smooth and strong as rolling thunder.

"My name, sir, is Alvin S. Ward. And all that you witness around you is mine."

Bear shoved his hat back and scratched his head. "Ya mean this town?"

"Yes!"

"I don't see why a sane man would want it."

"What? Did I hear you correctly, sir? Surely you jest. This . . . is . . . a . . . town."

"Towns have whiskey and women, mister. This place looks thin on both to me."

"Aha! Good point. But I do have whiskey, and the women will follow."

"How soon?" Bear asked.

"That may very well depend on the likes of you gentle-men. Yes, it may. Would you care to join me in a drink? I may have a golden opportunity for you."

"I'll settle for the whiskey," Zack said. "And that's plenty good enough."

The Great Whiskey Palace *was* impressive. As soon as Zack stepped inside, he heard Bear suck in his breath and then follow with a low whistle. Overhead, three monumental chandeliers lit the room. A long, hand-carved mahogany bar gleamed invitingly. There were two faro tables and a white piano. The boards underfoot were sanded and clean. And best of all, the liquor cabinet behind the bar was well stocked.

"I must be dreaming," Zack whispered reverently. He walked slowly across the floor until he came to the bar. Very carefully he reached out and touched the smooth wood. "It's real."

"I can see you are suitably impressed, gentlemen."

"Whoo-whee!" Bear yelled. "Pour me a drink."

Alvin S. Ward refilled their glasses one, final time. He leaned his elbows on the bar and seemed to measure them once again before speaking. "This place represents all that I own in the world. It is my fortune. But, as you can see, it is like a beautiful spinster woman. Unfilled and alone. It was not always like this. The lines around his mouth crimped. "No, gentlemen. Just seventeen months ago, The Great Whiskey Palace was filled with humanity. And my cash registers did runneth over. Then it happened."

"What happened?" Zack asked.

"The Overland Stage Company decided to reroute to Running Springs. Do you know what that means?"

"Not good for the town, huh?"

"Not good! My God, man, it was the death sentence. And this," he rasped, flinging his hand out in a sweeping motion, "all of this was only four months old."

"Not that unusual," Zack said. "Towns spring up in days, and die just as fast. The country is dotted with them. You can't change that, Ward."

"Oh, but that's where you are wrong. Wrong!"

"Zack ain't ever wrong, mister. Careful what you say."

The man laughed nervously. "I meant no offense to your friend. But, listen." He leaned closer. "What if the stage resumed its original route? What—what do you think would happen?"

"Town would probably come to life again," Zack said.

"Ah! Correct! I knew you were men of intelligence when I first saw you ride in. Now," he said, speaking faster, "Let's carry it a bit farther. You saw all these buildings. There's a general store, an eighteen-room hotel which could easily be expanded, a livery, newspaper office, saddle shop—"

"Whoa up. What's your point? I got eyes; all these places you mention are just so much firewood now."

"Yes. But can you imagine what their value would be if Snakegrass Junction was reborn? A fortune! Right here rests a fortune, my friends. And all that is required to possess it is . . . to . . . get . . . the . . . gawddamn . . . stage . . . back!"

"Huh," Bear chuckled. "Huh!"

Zack felt himself inwardly tighten, and his eyes narrowed shrewdly, "You got a proposition you're aworkin' up to. Get to it, Mr. Ward."

"Convince the Overland Stage Company to reroute back to Snakegrass Junction and the fortune is yours."

"All of it!"

"No," Ward said quickly. "But almost. I will deed you everything except The Great Whiskey Palace. Everything!"

"Damn," Bear grunted. "This is the only place I'd want."

But Zack wasn't so sure. It wasn't every day in his life that someone offered him a whole town, and that wasn't something to sniff at—even if the place was abandoned. Besides, this Alvin S. Ward fella didn't seem to be no dummy. Any man who could scrape together enough money to put up a joint like The Great Whiskey Palace had to have some business savvy. "Don't see how me and Bear could handle a whole town. We don't know nothing about towns. Don't even like 'em."

"Ha-ha, but you would if you *owned* it. Ask yourself, sir, what it is about towns you dislike?"

"The law. And the rules. Ain't that right, Bear?"

"Yep."

"Then . . . listen carefully. Then, what if there were no laws that *you* didn't want and no rules that *you* didn't set."

"You could do that?"

"Why, of course! Snakegrass Junction would be yours. You'd be the same as the mayor, the city council, and the sheriff all rolled into one. Gentlemen, you would have absolute power. Think of it! And besides," he pressed, "you wouldn't have to actually operate the flourishing businesses. You would lease them."

"What's that mean?"

"It means they pay you to use your buildings. All you'd do is sit on the boardwalk with your feet up on a hitching rail and a glass of whiskey in your fist and collect your payments."

"That's all?"

He lifted his hands palms up and smiled with all his golden teeth. "That's all."

"Whew," Bear breathed. "That's the best thing I've ever heard of, Zack. What have we got to lose?"

"Don't know yet. Maybe nothing, maybe our lives."

"Please, my friends," Ward sighed. "No one will lose their lives. All you would have to do is to destroy the bridge over the Shoshone River."

"That's all?"

"I think . . . yes, I think that would do it. Although perhaps you might have to repeat the work several times until the citizens of Running Springs gave up."

"It would go against their grain, huh?"

"Oh, more than that. It would kill their town within three months. In fact, if the stage rerouted back to *your* town, I would expect their merchants would come to you begging for their places of business."

Zack glanced sideways at his partner. A low, rumbling laughter started to crawl up his throat. Bear was grinning hugely. "As far as I'm concerned," Zack said, "that just cinches the duck. I don't much give a damn about the absolute power and all that, but I can't hardly think of a better thing than destroying Running Springs."

"How about pouring us another drink to seal the deal."

"Here you are, Bear. And Zack. To our fortune and success!"

Zack Woolsey left them several hours later. Curiously, he seemed unable to get drunk. He sauntered out into the main street and sat down right in the center of it. Under the starlight, he spent a long time sizing up his town. It took him well over an hour and he scooted around on the seat of his buckskins until he'd revolved a full circle.

Snakegrass Junction may be a ghost town now, he thought, but not for long. He and Bear would see to that. By winter, instead of freezing to death in Canada, they'd be here running things. Zack closed his eyes, feeling a little silly. But he imagined how it would sound with people raising hell, having a grand time of it. By God, his town wouldn't have no law at all. Be like the old days, when a man settled his own disputes without no strangers horning in.

"By damn," he chuckled, "we can do it! And we get to kill Running Springs in the bargain."

For no other reason, he began to laugh.

CHAPTER 7

Without being consciously aware of it, the citizens of Running Springs were subject to a semiweekly ritual. Every Tuesday and Thursday, shortly before three in the afternoon, they found themselves in the vicinity of the Antelope Hotel. Men would glance offhandedly at their watches and talk to one another in a rather distracted manner. Women would find themselves shopping without any real intent to buy. They were all waiting. Waiting for the Overland stage to come rushing around the east corner of Main Street.

The Overland stage was their sole link with the outer world of big cities, politics, and even foreign wars. And though they were proud of their frontier independence, they were dependent upon the eastern cities for the things they could not provide themselves.

A hunter holding a crumpled catalogue picture of a new Remington Arms rifle he'd ordered almost six weeks before. The general-store owner's wife trying not to look excited about the half dozen new lace-trimmed parasols she was certain her church club partners would adore. A beaten-looking farmer, his angular wife and two children huddled in the wagon. For him, his entire future seemed to hinge on a new hybrid wheat guaranteed to double his past year's output. Yes, dammit, it *had* to—or they'd have to pull stakes and leave. Where? He didn't know, but that was all right. The new seed would take care of everything. Thank God, too; they couldn't have faced another year like those past.

Three-thirty. Where the hell was the stage? It wasn't like

its crotchety old driver, Andy Carson, to keep folks waiting. The people milled around with growing impatience. The hunter kept glancing at the picture of his rifle, and the farmer held a grain of wheat between his thick forefinger and thumb. The advertisement said that the new strain was half again the size of ordinary seed. Said it in writing. Had to be true, then . . . didn't it?

Darby Buckingham watched the crowd with an interest that was not entirely impersonal. The stage would arrive with three boxes of hermetically sealed Cuban cigars. They cost twenty-five cents each; as much as a hired man earned in a day. If the people suspected his extravagance, it would cause quite a stir. Darby gave enough of them away so that they never did. In addition to the cigars, there would probably be a couple New York City papers. He'd read them cover to cover. Afterward, he'd sit and relive his favorite Broadway plays and the operas.

It was at those times he withdrew into himself. Alone in his room, he would smoke his cigars, sip the best brandy he could lay his hands on, and ask himself again why he'd come West. Was it worth it? Always, he reached the same conclusions. He'd left his New York City apartment to see the frontier as it truly existed. Perhaps, even, to go down in some future text as a historian. With the exception of his latest book, on Zeb Cather, Darby knew that none of his stories would survive him. Before he'd come to Running Springs, all his dime novels had been exaggerated, commercial rubbish. Stories that would exist no longer than the early-morning frost under the bright, climbing sun. So, yes, it was worth coming West. But, still, for a man who loved luxury, it was a genuine sacrifice.

Four-fifteen. Darby noticed that the townspeople had dropped all pretense. The women stopped pretending they were shopping. The men weren't even attempting to carry on conversation. Everyone was just waiting. He saw the gambler, Edward Hyder, emerge from the Concord Saloon. That was unusual. Hyder wore an immense wrapping around his neck. He seemed embarrassed by it and rarely ventured out into the street. Perhaps he'd also felt the growing expectancy of the crowd.

So far, Darby had been unable to figure out a way to trap the man. Hyder still played poker, and usually won, but as far as Darby could tell he won fairly and only small amounts. But, then, why should he get careless? With the six hundred dollars he'd made off the two old hunters, he could afford to play it safe. Darby wondered how long Dr. Sawyer would be able to keep Hyder from traveling. Certainly no more than a month. If he's guilty, Darby thought, I've got to figure out a way to prove it—and soon.

At six o'clock and the sunlight fading, the people seemed to say, "The hell with it." The farmer whipped his team harder than was called for and snapped crossly at his wife as they left town. In the dirt where he'd waited, a small cluster of wheat seeds lay shredded. The general store closed a half hour early, and the saloons did a lousy business that night. There wasn't a damn thing to talk about and the people went to bed early. But, the next day, everything changed.

The stage arrived at midmorning, while Darby was still lingering over his morning coffee with Dolly Beavers. They, like everyone else in town, had been discussing yesterday's mystery.

"Speaking of the devil," Dolly rushed, "here's the stage!"

Before they even reached the street, Darby saw that people had surrounded Andy Carson.

"Get back, dammit. This is my stage and I'm responsible for it!" Andy Carson raised his whip meanacingly. The crowd recoiled. Andy's reputation was known to all. He was cantankerous, crotchety, and totally unpredictable. He drove a stage because people in general gave him a pain in the ass. Most people would step into the street to avoid passing him.

"Take it easy, Mr. Carson," Darby called. "These people are simply concerned for you and your passengers. We—"

"Buffalo balls, Derby Man! If I pitched over dead out there, they'd curse me for delaying their mail and packages."

"Perhaps," Darby said, suppressing a grin, "we better take a walk over to the office and you can tell me what happened."

"Can't. I'm behind schedule almost ten hours."

"I have to go to the powder room," came a protesting voice from inside.

Carson twisted around and smashed the lead-filled whip handle against the roof of the coach three times, hard. "Lady, I don't give—"

"Mr. Carson!" Darby roared. All eyes revolved to him. "Mr. Carson, as acting sheriff I insist that you join me in my office. Now."

"But I told you. My schedule—"

"Hang your schedule!" Darby saw a heavy young man starting to climb out. "My wife has to go to the powder room. Surely you wouldn't refuse her call of nature."

"Of course he wouldn't," Darby soothed. He glanced up at the driver. "While these people are accommodated and a fresh team is harnessed, we can be talking. I won't detain you any longer than that."

Carson nodded grimly. "Ten hours, fourteen hours. What the hell does it matter? The Company can't get any madder than they already will be." He swung down and followed Darby to the Sheriff's Office.

Darby shut the door behind them. The office smelled of stale air. He didn't like the place. It was just a square brick room with a crude set of bars across the rear third of the interior. Everything about the room fit the image of Sheriff Zeb Cather. The gun rack, the fly-specked WANTED posters, the stark functionalism. And there wasn't a book in sight. Thank heavens, Darby thought, I haven't had to jail anyone longer than a few hours. He was sure no prisoner would find the confinement more odious than he.

"You've got yourself a problem, Derby Man."

Darby plopped down behind the desk and motioned Andy Carson to take the chair across from him. "Were you robbed?"

"Hell, no. Sidetracked! That's what I was. Someone destroyed the bridge over the Shoshone."

Darby's eyebrows raised. It had been Andy Carson who'd driven the stage that had taken him West. Darby searched back to that time and recalled that the bridge itself was really nothing more than a space of huge logs supported by two pilings. At this time of year, the Shoshone River was formidable enough to make the bridge of vital importance.

"How did they do it?"

"Well, it took some work, I can tell you. Wasn't no kids or Indians larkin' around. They took axes and chopped the logs away from the far bank. Musta been a hell of a job. Then they really fixed it good. From the tracks down by the water it was plain enough that they musta pulled the cut logs down using horses and ropes."

"Can it be repaired?"

"Sure. But it won't be easy. Those cut logs are as big around as you are. No offense," he said quickly.

"None taken," Darby replied abruptly.

"And they're all hanging down in the water every which way. Like as if a herd of beavers decended on 'em for a picnic. Be a hell of a job to fix up."

"How much time do we have?"

"Well, let's see. Today is Friday. Because, see, I should have been here yesterday, which was—"

"I know. I know."

"Then, you figure it out. Next stage is due on Tuesday. But I won't be driving it."

"Why not?"

"Well, the schedule is blown. They'll put a relief driver on. Guess I'll have to go clear to Salt Lake City with this one. I'm going to go over to the telegraph office and find out. But I know what they'll say. If that bridge isn't passable, they'll order the next man to reroute to Snakegrass Junction."

"Why would they do that?"

"Dammit, you don't know much for being sheriff, do you?"

"Humor me and simply respond to my questions," Darby said, impatience rising in his voice.

Andy shifted uncomfortably. "I guess nobody ever told you the story. For many years, Snakegrass Junction was on the stage line. Then the Overland Stage Company decided to bypass Snakegrass and come directly here. They did it for good reason, too. In fact, I helped talk 'em into it."

"And kill Snakegrass, I presume."

"Needed killing," the driver protested. "The town went rotten. A man named Alvin S. Ward arrived. He had a lot of money. A lot. Wasn't six months before he bought the little people out and built the grandest saloon I ever set foot in. But he was the most double-dealin' son of a bitch I ever saw."

"In what way?"

"You name it, he did it, as long as there was a dollar to be made. Bought out the livery and raised his prices to the sky. My teams of horses were fed bad hay. Lost two of 'em in the traces, from the colic."

Andy stood and began to pace back and forth across the room. Anger rose in his voice. "And my passengers fared no better. In the morning when it was time to pull out, I was always missing somebody. A few, I never found. And those I did had mostly been beaten and robbed at night. Finally, they picked on the wrong man. Some eastern fella, like you. Said he had over a thousand dollars taken from under his mattress. He raised a hell of a stink over it, and Mr. Ward just laughed in his face. A mistake. I don't know what that city man did when he got to San Francisco. But it must have been plenty. Wasn't two weeks later the Company ordered me to pass Snakegrass Junction and come here. I reckon Alvin Ward went wild. Heard he rode back East to try and get the Company to change its mind. But they never did. That crooked bastard had already slit his throat and the town's right along with it."

"So the town died. Where did this Alvin S. Ward go next?"

Andy Carson moved up to the desk and leaned closer. "That's the strange part," he whispered. "Ward didn't go nowhere. He stayed!"

"In an abandoned town?"

"Yep. Yesterday, when I saw we couldn't get across the Shoshone, I decided to head for Snakegrass. Hell, I had to backtrack downriver anyway. I figured if worse came to worst and I had to, we could always unload and hole up for the night while the horses rested. But when we got to Snakegrass, damned if they weren't waiting for us!"

"They? You said they."

"That's right. Alvin S. Ward himself and two of the roughest old devils I ever saw in my life. You know what I think?"

Darby sighed deeply. He didn't want to hear what Andy Carson thought. He'd pieced it all together himself and it spelled trouble. "Zack Woolsey and Bear Timberly," he muttered.

"Huh?"

"Never mind. Tell me what you think."

"Last Tuesday, those same two tried to block the bridge. I run 'em off into the river. Gawddamn, you shoulda seen me! You shoulda seen the faces on them two uglies when they went flying."

"I think I can imagine. And you say the same pair were in Snakegrass Junction last night?"

"That's right. The tall one, when he first saw me I thought

he was going to go for our rifles. But, before it happened, that gold-toothed skunk Alvin S. Ward, he jumped in between us and started pumpin' my paw like I was his long-lost blood brother. Tellin' me how Snakegrass Junction was at our . . . how did he put that?"

"Disposal?"

"That's right. How'd you know?"

"Just a guess. Then what happened?"

"Well, the tall one, he just stomped away looking like he'd got sick on green apples. Then the other two, Ward and the hairy fella, they took us into the Whiskey Palace and said all drinks were free as long as we stayed."

"Doesn't sound like the same man you described earlier."

"The hell it doesn't! Ain't hard to figure out his angle. He wants the Overland Stage Company's business. But I showed him! Told him to go to hell. I paid for my whiskey or I wouldn't drink."

"How did he react?"

"You mean what did he do?"

"Yes. That's what I mean."

Andy frowned and shook his head slowly. "That's the part that bothered me. He didn't get mad or nothing. Just said that he understood and wanted to make up for hard feelings. I hated it when he did that. What can a man do? Two years ago he would have hired someone to kill me. Yesterday it was like he'd got religion."

"Perhaps he really did change."

"Sure. And perhaps the bridge just happened to cut itself in half. About as likely. I'll tell you what I'm thinking. I'm thinking he's got those two old rawhiders working for him. I'd bet it was they that wrecked the bridge."

It was the same conclusion Darby had reached five minutes earlier. Zack and Bear hated Running Springs. Obviously this Alvin S. Ward had no love for it either. Somehow, then, ill fate had conspired to bring the trio together. Darby ground his teeth in exasperation. What a mess!

He glanced up at Andy Carson. The man was obviously waiting for him to confirm his suspicions. "It's possible you are correct. However, it's also possible the bridge was destroyed by someone else."

"What? That's crazy! What kind of a sheriff are you, anyway? Do you think someone went to all that work for the fun of it? Maybe they was just bored. Huh?"

It wasn't going to work with the man, Darby thought. "Look," he began. "To be perfectly honest—I agree with you."

"You do? Then, why didn't you say so in the first place? I was beginning to think you was thickheaded."

"To make a short answer, those two men were here a few days and I suspect they were cheated out of six hundred dollars. So they have a reason to want to get even with this town. I mishandled the affair. I sincerely hope I can correct the situation and return them their money. But, even more important, I believe that until I have evidence that Zack and Bear are behind this, I must contain my suspicions."

"But . . . but why?"

"Can you imagine what the town would do if it understood the real motive underneath all this? A lynch mob. And believe me, Mr. Carson, I don't yet know what kind of man this Alvin Ward is, but those two others are not to be taken lightly. I think they'd open up on a group of riders before they ever reached Snakegrass. People would die needlessly. I don't want that, do you?"

"Damn," Carson swore. "It's a lot more complicated than I figured. Anything I can do to help?"

"No, not now. Just keep your—no, our . . . our suspicions quiet. By the time you return, we'll have the bridge repaired and the stage back on schedule to Running Springs."

"I hope so. That Ward fella makes me sick! The other two aren't much better. They was saying they owned the town and wanted to make it nice for my passengers. God, they was almost gushy." He took a deep breath. "But I'll have to admit, they'd cleaned up the hotel rooms and hauled in water for washing ourselves. Next morning, everyone said they'd slept good. And not a one was robbed."

Darby gathered himself and rose from his chair. "You'd better be rolling. And don't worry. We have almost four days until the next stage is due in. By then, the bridge will be repaired and everything will be back to normal. When you telegraph your employer, be sure and relay that. You have my word."

"From what I hear from folks, that's good enough. So long."

Almost before the stage left town, Darby had an office full of people. There were Dr. Sawyer, half the merchants, and even Dolly Beavers. All were furious and said as much. They'd lost money, and that was inexcusable. To a person, they'd heard the story from Andy's passengers and had put two and two together. It took all the persuasiveness he possessed to calm them down. And even so, when he'd finally gotten rid of everyone except Dolly, he sensed that they had departed in anger.

"Well," he growled, "what do you have left to say that they didn't?"

"Darby, honey," she said. "Don't be cross with me."

She walked around behind him, placed her hands upon his shoulders and began to massage. "You're upset. I can tell. All your muscles are tight."

"Well—"

"Why don't you just sit quiet and relax, dear? This is Dolly, remember?"

Darby remembered. There were times, like now, when she was the best thing he'd ever had. Dolly could be an angel or a smiling and beguiling vixen. Warm, sensuous, and caring. But there were occasions, he thought, when she could drive him almost insane with nonstop chatter. Those were the times when he just wanted to yell, "Stop!" But they were rare. So he just shut his eyes and let her fingers roll away the tension. Being sheriff was hard and thankless.

"You must forgive them," she was saying. "The stage means so much to this town. Most of us really depend on the passengers for our livelihood. I'm sure you will do the right thing." The fingers stopped moving. "What will you do, Darby?"

He groaned. The fun was over. "Look, Dolly, I'm going to ride over to look at the bridge and then go on to Snakegrass Junction."

"On a horse?"

"What else?"

She wisely chose not to pursue the answer. "Then what?"

"I'll talk to them. State my suspicions and get their promise it won't happen again. It's . . . as easy as that." He snapped his fingers.

"Darby, honey." She cleared her throat. It was a signal he knew well. It meant she disagreed, so he didn't let her get started.

"I'm the sheriff. It's my job. Besides, those two men aren't killers. You know that as well as I do."

"But they're not exactly reasonable men, are they?"

Darby walked over to the gun rack and pulled out the shotgun that Zeb had taught him to use.

"Don't worry." He kissed her. She tried to hold him, but he pulled away. "I'll be back after dark," he said going out the door.

"You know where to find me," she said.

For the first time that day, he smiled.

Darby rode out of town the back way. He was a poor horseman and knew it. It had occurred to him that the sight of their sheriff bouncing off his horse wouldn't inspire the least bit of confidence among the townsfolk. He hated horses. The barbarous Mongols that had pillaged Europe had probably liked horses. No doubt Attila the Hun had thought of them as a superior form of transportation. Darby bounced along thinking about how little mankind had progressed in some areas. A coach and driver. That was the only civilized form of travel.

Thank heavens, he thought, the Shoshone River Bridge isn't far. Only about seven miles. Then another ten miles to Snakegrass Junction. Seventeen miles. Still wasn't bad until he considered that was *each* way. "Thirty-four miles," he grunted. "Not so good."

He checked his watch and was surprised to see that it was already two o'clock. There was no help for it. He took a firm grip on the saddle horn and forced his mount into a gallop. The experience was just as agonizing as he'd remembered.

The bridge was even worse than Andy Carson had described. Darby tied his horse to a patch of thickets and walked up to the structure. On his side, the bridge hadn't been touched. All the damage was on the other end. He stepped out onto the bridge and started across for a better look.

There was no danger of the logs collapsing underfoot. One didn't need to be a bridge builder to see that the whole thing rested squarely on the two supporting piles. Darby approached the center and peered over the side. His first impression was of the power of the current below. He remembered Andy Carson saying that he'd run Zack and Bear over the side. Darby shook his head. It was a wonder they hadn't drowned. The roar of water filled his ears and he studied the pilings underneath. Actually, he saw, each piling consisted of two huge logs bound together with chain. Even so, up above, he could feel a faint swaying. Probably because the bridge had lost its support against the far bank. He straightened up and cautiously walked forward until he came to the point where the logs slanted down at an angle. "Thunder and lightning," he swore. "What a mess!"

And indeed it was. The current had twisted the logs until there was no form or direction at all. He saw gaps where the timber had been swept away entirely. Without question, he wasn't going to be able to get his horse across. It would be a very risky undertaking just to cross by himself. He'd have to tightrope across the logs, hoping his weight did not dislodge them. A foolish risk with nothing to gain. He surely wasn't going to walk the last ten miles to Snakegrass.

Darby sat down and drew out a cigar. As long as he wasn't going to have to ride any farther, there was no sense in hurrying. The thing to do now was to try and figure out how to repair the bridge as fast as possible. Let's see. There were eleven logs across. The distance from the center support pilings to the far bank had to be at least sixty feet, maybe even sixty-five. Atop the pilings was a wide support, notched and intact, for the eleven timbers. No problem there. All they'd have to do is get a couple men on the far bank and slide the replacement logs across. When he finished his cigar, he'd pace off the distance he'd walked from the center to the west bank; then he'd know exactly how long they'd have to be.

He struck a match to his cigar. The cigar exploded in his fingers as a bullet whined by. Darby rolled sideways across the logs, expecting the next one to tear into him at any moment. He yanked out his derringer and felt like a fool who surely deserved to die. What good was a blasted derringer!

Another shot and he saw a puff of smoke filter out of some bushes on the far bank about thirty yards upriver. Darby's attention swung around behind him. Horrified, he saw his horse at least one hundred yards from where he'd tied it. The reins were trailing on the ground. The beast had run, then apparently stepped on them and brought himself up short.

"Treacherous ambushers!" he shouted in fury. The roar of

the water below was so loud he knew they couldn't hear him. He had to get away. His position was indefensible. Darby gathered his legs under him, jumped up, and ran.

He was halfway across when he heard another shot. He actually saw the dirt kick up between his horse's forefeet. The animal whinnied in fear and went racing away. "Stop, damn you!"

A shot blew his hat neatly off his head. Darby cleared the bridge and dived for brush and safety.

He lay still for almost an hour. A dense cloud of gnats hovered over his head and were a dead giveaway. They buzzed in his ears and before his eyes. One flew up his nostril. He choked and decided he'd rather risk getting shot than going insane. He stood up swearing and shaking his fist at the place across the river where he'd seen the powder smoke. There was no answering shot. Nothing but the river sound.

Darby picked up his derby hat and inspected the holes in front and back. Whoever had been shooting hadn't meant to kill, that much was certain. Anyone who could hit a cigar, even a fat one such as he smoked, at that distance had to be a rare marksman. Darby shoved the hat down over his forehead until it pinched.

He started for town. There wasn't a doubt in his mind that the marksmen had been Zack Woolsey and Bear Timberly. True, he had no proof but, blast! he'd had all he was going to take.

CHAPTER 8

Darby Buckingham trudged over the prairie in a black mood. To make matters worse, the damned horse never left his sight. The contrary animal seemed intent on staying just far enough ahead to provoke him. Its pattern became predictable during the first mile. Always, he would nearly reach it, only to have the nag suddenly shy away as if startled and race ahead to resume feeding. To the horse, the day's outing was a game.

They were both going back to town. Darby cursed the animal and prayed that it would at least be merciful enough to spare him the indignity of galloping up Main Street. If he had been in possession of a rifle, he would not have hesitated to shoot the miserable beast.

Daylight passed and the stars appeared. He stopped for a moment to dig a cigar from his vest pocket. Crushed! It must have happened when he'd leapt for cover. He lifted his arms to the sky in a beseeching gesture, then dropped them to his sides and continued on. In the darkness he could barely see the horse up ahead. At least, he thought, the beast will lead me in the right direction. A man could get lost.

As the miles passed, he debated what action to take against Bear and Zack. His first impulse was to retaliate. Those two scoundrels must be taught a sound lesson. They had wounded his pride and caused him to appear a fool. That was unforgivable. Yet, he had to admit that he dared not take the issue personally. The two hunters had suffered financially and probably felt they were justified in their actions. No, he decided, I represent the law and my first responsibility is to the town. And that meant seeing that the bridge was ready for next week's stage. First things first, he told himself. Repair the bridge and then go to Snakegrass Junction.

At last he saw the winking lights of Running Springs. "Please, horse, take the back way to your feedbag. Don't do this to me."

His heart almost wept with gratitude when the animal trotted straight for the barn. Ten minutes later, he had unsaddled and poured it an extra measure of oats. The horse had spared him a great, final indignity. Not a man to hold a grudge, he made peace. After all, he reasoned, he would have to ride tomorrow and he decided it would be wiser to part amicably.

Darby avoided Main Street and reached the Antelope Hotel without detection. He climbed the stairs, feeling totally exhausted. On tiptoes he reached his room and fitted the key. Bed and blessed sleep. The day had been a nightmare. Tomorrow promised to be no better.

"Darby, honey!"

A long sigh escaped his lips. He would have fled, but he had nowhere to go. "Please, not tonight."

"You look terrible! What happened?"

He collapsed into a chair and related the entire wretched story while she kept his brandy glass full. "I'd better let you get some sleep," she said when it was over.

At the door, she blew him a kiss. "I think you're right about getting the bridge fixed. And don't feel so badly about what happened today. I'm just thankful they didn't try to kill you."

"They could have, Dolly. It's a terrible feeling being that helpless. I've never been in a situation like that before."

Dolly watched him for a long minute before speaking. "If you go to Snakegrass Junction alone, you might not be so lucky a second time. I know their type, Darby. They probably think this is some kind of game. It won't always be that way with them. Like the children they are, they'll quickly tire of the game. When they do, I'm afraid of what will happen."

"Do you have so little faith in me?"

"No," she whispered.

In the hallway light, he saw her face grow sad. It shocked him, because he'd never seen her look at him that way. "Dolly, I'll be fine. I can take care of myself."

"They won't fight you with their fists again," she said. "What you don't seem to understand is that, when you ride out there, you'll be in their element. They'll have every advantage. Darby?"

"Yes."

"Promise me you won't go alone. I know of at least twenty men who—"

"Who would start shooting at the slightest provocation," he snapped. Darby rubbed his hand over his face wearily and eased his head back onto his pillow. "Didn't mean to sound so harsh. But I have to take care of this by myself."

"I know," she said. "And that's why I'm so worried for you. Good night, dear."

It took them three days, sunup to sundown, to repair the bridge. The work was hard and dangerous. The entire first day was devoted simply to clearing away the fallen timber. They had to cut the connected ends free from the center pilings and then remove the logs that were hung up on the bank. They rolled them into the current and they were swept away downriver. The second day, they picked eleven big pines, cut them down, and trimmed them. Darby swung his ax until the palms of his hands blistered and bled. He watched with grim satisfaction as the logs were chained and dragged to the river by three teams of stout horses. As he'd expected, the placement was not difficult. The logs were hauled out onto the center of the bridge. Ropes were tied to the ends and thrown over the water to riders on the far side. At a single command, the horsemen began to pull the logs across the gap until they were secure on the far bank. They used wedges to lift each timber into place and secure them firmly. At last, they were finished.

"Twenty-four hours to spare," Darby said.

"What makes you think they won't do it again?" Wallace Henley said out loud. Around him, the other men nodded the same question.

"He's right," said a heavy-set man whom Darby had recognized as the owner of the Bulldog Saloon. "Take them three hours to destroy it and half the town three days to fix it again."

Darby raised his hand for silence. "We'll post guards. At least for the first week."

"Who the hell has got time?"

Darby bristled. "Who wants to see the stage go to Snakegrass Junction tomorrow?"

Before he left, Darby posted two guards. One at each end of the bridge. It was best, he thought, to take no chances.

"Well," Zack said, "there they go. The whole damn bunch of 'em feeling everything is going to be all right." A smile creased his face as he turned to Bear. "Jesus, are they going to be steamin' tomorrow!"

"What about the guards?"

"Yeah, I hadn't expected that. No matter," he said. Zack glanced up at the sun. "Be dark in only three or four more hours. That's when we move. I'll ride upriver and swim my horse across. You sneak in on this side. When I do my wildbird call, that means we take 'em."

"I don't know, Zack."

"What don't you know?"

Bear took a long time answering. "Well, I'd rather you didn't do the bird call. It don't sound so good."

"It what!"

"Sounds more like . . . like a sick fox to me."

Zack bit off a hunk of chewing tobacco and chewed rapidly. A sick fox, huh? After all these years there were still times he reckoned he hardly knew Bear Timberly. It was a mean thing he'd said.

"Why don't you croak like a frog, Zack? That one's passable."

"All right," he snapped. "The frog sound. When you hear me, croak back so's I know you're ready. And listen, don't hurt the guard, and don't let him see you. That's the most important thing. If we take 'em unawares, that Darby Buckingham won't have any way to pin it on us."

Bear nodded. He seemed sleepy. "I ain't looking forward to all that work we got ahead of us. Chopping logs all night is mighty hard."

"Truly. But just think of the looks on their faces when they find out that *both* ends of the bridge have been hacked off."

"That'd be something worth paying for." Bear stretched out to wait.

From their hiding place upriver, Zack could see the two guards talking on the middle of the bridge. They were town people and, therefore, didn't pose any great threat. In fact, if there wasn't so much timber to chop, he'd probably have decided to just kill time until they fell asleep. He was sure they would.

Zack studied the far bank until he knew exactly how he'd make his approach. He'd tie his horse in the aspens and move in low to the ground. He was a hunter and there would be no sound. Hell, with the river rambling by, he could go in singing and not be heard. The whole thing would be so easy as to take the fun out of it.

Once he had almost reached the guard, he'd do his frog sound and move in. The guard wouldn't know what hit him. He'd be trussed up and blindfolded almost before he hit the ground. If they'd been facing an Indian hunting party or a couple of mountain men, it would be something worth planning. This, however, would be as easy as falling asleep.

The sun dived toward the hills and Zack waited patiently. The guards weren't even worth watching, he thought. If they'd half a brain they would have taken cover on both banks and kept out of sight. Instead, they stood together spittin' and smoking over the Shoshone and not doing nothing except making themselves a perfect target.

The real fun would probably come tomorrow. Zack figured there would be a lynch party come busting over to Snakegrass Junction. Whether or not there would be a shooting all depended on Sheriff Buckingham. If the townsfolk overrode him, some folks were going to get ventilated. On the other hand, if the man somehow managed to keep them under control, maybe it would be different.

He recognized that they were putting Buckingham in a bad spot. If everything went as planned tonight, the sheriff still wouldn't have a shred of proof. His hands would be tied. Proof. That's the excuse he'd used to save the gambler's hide. Well, it would sure as the devil be interesting to see if it worked both ways.

Zack moved away to the horses. He pulled two axes from their packs and rummaged around until he found a whetstone. In the fading light, he worked on the axes and listened to Bear snore peacefully until it was time to start.

"Wake up, I'm going off now. Should take me no more than an hour. You be listening, hear?" Bear yawned sleepily and he rode off. A mile above the bridge, Zack found a wide spot and urged his horse into the water. God, it was cold! His horse went to its withers and then Zack felt the animal strike out swimming. They made it to the other side without mishap. Ten minutes later he was in position near the water.

He cupped his hands around his lips and took a lungful of air, "Crock-it. Crock-it." He listened.

Not more than a dozen feet away came an answering "Croak-up. Croak-up." Zack swore. A real frog. Then an-

other. Soon the entire west bank began to join in the chorus.
He leaned out over the water, trying to hear Bear. He
called again, much louder. "Crock-it! Crock-it!"

What sounded like a thousand frogs took up the song.

"Jesus!" he swore in disgust. No matter how much a man
planned it out, something was sure to ball things up. There
was no way of knowing what Bear was doing.

Zack began to creep toward the guard. There was just
enough light to see him. The man was leaning against a tree.
The bright orange dot from his cigarette was like a guiding
light. Zack circled around behind, placing each moccasined
foot down carefully. It really wasn't necessary. The frogs
were going wild down near the water. Damnedest racket he'd
ever heard in his life. To make that kind of noise, some of 'em
had to be as big as turtles.

When he was within a yard of the man, Zack grunted like
a grizzly bear. The guard started to turn and Zack hit him
squarely in the temple. He felt the blow clear up his arm and
knew he'd delivered a knockout punch. The man crashed
down. He didn't even twitch.

Zack rubbed his knuckles proudly. Be damned if he hadn't
done that right. Hope Bear doesn't foul his end of it, he
thought. He pulled a long length of leather strip from around
his waist. Within minutes the unconscious man was bound up
tighter than a papoose.

Zack stood erect and peered across the river. How was
Bear doing? He sat down to wait. Gradually, the frogs began
to settle down. There was no stick-to-it in frogs, he decided.
When the last croak died, Zack decided something must have
gone wrong on Bear's end. He should have been here by now
with the axes. What the devil could have happened? There
hadn't been any gunfire.

He decided he'd have to cross the bridge. Zack didn't like
that. If, by some accident, the guard was still waiting, Zack
knew he'd be a perfect target out over the water. There

would be no place to go except into the river. He didn't want that. Damn Bear, anyway! he raged.

Zack started across the bridge on his hands and knees. Every foot he traveled, the tension grew. He passed over the center of the bridge and kept going. Another forty feet. He began to crawl faster. If he could just make the other side and get into the thickets. . . .

A match flared. Zack flattened. He pressed his entire length down into the groove where the logs joined. His heart pounded and he dared not even look up. He heard a cough nearby. It wasn't Bear.

Very slowly, he raised his head until he could see. At first, he was unable to spot the guard. Then the cigarette glowed brightly and Zack recognized the indistinct form. He began to inch forward. There wasn't a doubt in his mind that he would be able to overpower the man. Zack had the element of surprise, and the darkness was in his favor. But what if the jasper recognized him before falling? Zack swallowed hard and found he was sweating. If the guard could identify him, the game was up. The writing sheriff would have the proof he needed. Everything would be lost. He and Bear would never own their own town.

This is it, then, Zack thought. If I mess this up, it's back to Canada. Either that or the guard would have to die. Damn that Bear! It's his fault I'm faced with this!

He was close now. Underneath, Zack could feel the water surge against the pilings, and the faint trembling that ran up through the logs pressed against his body. He hadn't felt it before. Twenty feet at most. The guard's foot scraped on the logs. He was coming! Why?

Footsteps sounded faintly on the logs. Zack reached down and grasped the bone handle of his skinning knife. He started to slide it out of its sheath. Then he pushed it back. This was not self-defense. It would be murder. Zack rolled sideways and eased his body over the edge of the bridge. He dug his fingers into the bark of the logs and slowly lowered until he felt the current bite into his legs, pull him, chill him.

The strain on his arms and shoulders grew. The water was up to his thighs and it wanted to tear him away and send him churning under the bridge. Zack saw the form clearly now. It had stopped. The guard stood no more than ten feet away. If he looked down, Zack knew he'd have to fall into the water to avoid being recognized. What the hell was he waiting for!

Suddenly, the orange tip of a cigarette arched into the blackness and Zack saw it spark into the water. Just as quickly, the silhouette spun around and disappeared from the bridge. Zack figured maybe it was too late. He was shaking so badly from the strain, he didn't believe he could pull himself up. He rested his forehead against the bark and took several deep breaths. Then he threw his body up. He got one elbow on the top. He stretched out with his other arm and felt his fingers bite into wood. He pulled with his elbow, his arm, and even dug his bony chin into the top of the log and heaved with all the muscles in his neck. He made it.

For long minutes, he lay still. Gradually, his tremors ceased. He rocked to his feet and, crouching low, covered the last of the distance until he felt himself on ground. Zack was all business now. Already he'd wasted too much time, thanks to Bear. Up ahead, he heard the man. Zack glided forward on his moccasined feet and did not make a sound. Then he saw him standing by a tree, staring up at the stars. Zack closed in swiftly, his fist chopped, thudded into the base of the guard's neck.

He looked down at his quarry. Well, Zack thought, if he wanted to see stars, I gave him his wish. He didn't have any more leather strings to tie him, so Zack unbuckled the guard's belt and pulled it free. Next, he drew out his knife and cut the belt lengthwise. He was able to tie him hand and foot.

Zack stood up and surveyed his work with satisfaction. It would do. Now, where the hell was Bear?

He was sleeping. Zack found him exactly where they'd parted several hours earlier. For almost a full minute, the tall man stood over his partner, debating what to do. He watched Bear's lips pucker back and forth with each breath. It was hard for Zack to stay mad at his friend. After all, he thought, anyone could fall asleep. So, after thinking about it, he simply took Bear's hat, filled it with cold river water, and carried it over to the man. He bent close to Bear's ear. "Crock-it! Crock-it!" he bellowed. "Crock-it, God damn you!"

Bear jackknifed erect and Zack shoved the hatful of water right into his face. Blindly, Bear lashed out. Zack leaned back just in time, then slapped the shaggy head, once, twice, very hard.

Still half asleep, Bear came up fighting and Zack leapt away. A blow from the huge man could be disabling.

"What . . . Zack! Did you do that?"

"Yep." He saw Bear blink, shake his head back and forth.

"My ears are ringing, damn you!"

"I oughta slice them off. While you were sleeping, I had to get both the guards. Now we've got work to do and we're late starting." Without another word, Zack grabbed an ax and started for the bridge.

He was halfway across before Bear caught up with him, breathing fast. Bear trotted right by without a word. But when he reached the bank, Zack saw his ax flash in the moonlight and heard it dig into the logs. In less than a heartbeat, the ax slashed again and he saw ivory wood chips fly. Zack took a position over the other outside log and hefted his own ax. Bear was mad. That's good, Zack thought. He'll work a hell of a lot harder. He raised his ax and began the stroke that he knew would only be half as fast as Bear's for the first hour. There was plenty of time, almost six hours before sunrise.

And when they'd finished, the whole blamed bridge would be firewood.

Sun crawled over the land. One minute, only a faint white line against the eastern contour of the world; the next minute, glowing like fire on the hills. Zack Woolsey and Bear Timberly sat smoking their pipes and watched the day begin. This morning was special because they wanted to see the extent of their night's destruction. When the light grew stronger, they were both struck with wonder.

Below them, the Shoshone River Crossing was nothing but a gigantic rat's nest of timber. Logs twisted and missing. Everything gone. And, in the very center, Zack saw the central pilings with logs hanging from them. It looked to him like a huge half-assed tepee lodge out there. He chuckled softly. "It's a hell of a job we've done. A hell of a job!"

"Wish we could have cut down those pilings."

"It doesn't matter. Besides, I kind of favor the effect. And if we'd have been able to cut it all away, they'd be able to start clean. My guess is that they'll spend a good week just clearing the river. My, oh, my, we're better than a colony of beavers." He stood up and stretched his aching muscles. "We should be heading out before those guards wake."

Bear laughed. "Sure wish we could stay and see the look on the stagecoach driver's face."

"Yeah," Zack added. "And I hope it's that blamed Andy Carson, that run us off the bridge. If it wasn't for Ward, I'd have taken Carson apart the day he drove into our town. Let's ride."

Bear started for his horse.

"Great grizzly! My horse," Zack wailed.

"What's wrong with him?"

"He ain't here!"

"Where'd he go?" Bear asked, spinning around in a full circle.

"I left him on the other side."

Bear shook his head sorrowfully. He gathered his reins and swung into the saddle. "You're getting forgetful in your old age, Zack. I seen it happen before." He gigged his horse toward the river. "Don't know how you'd survive out here without me," he said, riding off.

Zack reached down and hefted a rock. He saw Bear's horse jump at the water. Zack dropped the rock by his side and smiled. Maybe it was good that Bear saw him make a mistake. After all, I'm a human too, he conceded.

A. S. Ward stood waiting on the street before the Great Whiskey Palace. "Look at him, just standing there with his hands on his hips," Bear complained. "Why wasn't he out there all night chopping logs with us?"

"'Cause he ain't a working man," Zack said.

"Well, hell! That makes him better'n you and me?"

"Nope. Didn't say that. But don't let him bother you. He's the man with the ideas and money. There's some in this world who use their wits rather than muscle. That's the kind he is."

A. S. Ward waved and began to walk toward them. "Do you cotton to him?" Bear asked.

"Nope."

"Well, do you trust him?"

"Hell no!"

"Then, why—"

Zack spoke quickly. "What he and us can do together don't require trust or likin'. It's simple. We need each other and that's as good a way to work a deal as any, I'd say. But when the time comes that man can do without us, we better watch our backs."

"How will we know?"

"We'll know," Zack said. "Howdy, Ward. It's nice to see you up early frettin' about Bear and me."

A thin smile played at the corners of Ward's mouth, then disappeared. "How did you gentlemen fare?"

"We did it," Zack said.

"No . . . ah, complications?"

"Yeah, there were a couple. But if you mean, did anyone recognize us, the answer is no."

This time the smile was broad. "Good! Excellent! That's precisely what I wanted to hear." Sunlight glinted off his gold teeth. "You two did a fine job. It deserves a round of whiskey. Put your horses up in my livery and come—"

"Our livery," Zack corrected.

"Huh?"

"It belongs to Bear and me." He swept his long arm out. "Everything except the Whiskey Palace, remember?"

Zack saw the muscles around A. S. Ward's eyes spasm. The eyelids drooped just a fraction. Zack filed these observations away. When the time arrived that Ward decided they were no longer useful, those facial hints might be very important. They might make the difference between being alive— and being dead.

"Yes. Yes, of course. Your livery, and town." A. S. Ward pivoted on his heel and stalked away, calling back over his shoulder, "Drinks are still on me in my establishment."

"You ruffled him, Zack."

"I know. He's touchy about this place. Let's put these horses away and drink some of his whiskey, then go to *our* hotel and get some sleep."

"Yeah. It's a fair place. Fancier than the Antelope Hotel in Running Springs, even."

"That's right," Zack said. "All it lacks is the bountiful Miss Dolly Beavers herself."

"Could be we could fix that."

Zack chuckled. "Funny, Bear, how our minds run down the same trails. But, first things first. I'm curious to see what Ward has got planned next. Let's go."

Alvin S. Ward sat relaxed and waiting. On his table stood a

bottle and glasses. He motioned them to help themselves. Zack poured and leaned back to listen.

"How long do you think the bridge will be out?" Ward asked.

"Hard to say," Zack said. "We figure two weeks, maybe three. They'll have to start from the beginning."

"Good." He pursed his lips in thought. "My friends, I believe we'll need at least three more weeks to convince the Overland Stage Company that Snakegrass Junction should again become the staging point for all its traffic in this part of Wyoming."

"How do we convince them of anything?" Zack asked.

"Two ways. I grease a few wheels in the Company with money. Perhaps buy out the stagecoach driver." He winked. "You know what I mean. It's called promotional expense. Very effective."

"It's called a pay-off," Zack grunted. "And with Andy Carson it won't work."

"It might." Their eyes locked. "Zack, it would help if you treated him civil."

"Look. Forget him. He won't play your game. If you try to buy Carson, he'll spit in your face and go high-tailing it to Running Springs. The whole town will know the story."

"Hmmm. Perhaps you are right. After all, you know the type better than I."

Zack took a glance at Bear. He'd missed the insult completely and that was just as well. Zack decided to let it pass.

"What I want to know," Bear said slowly, "is what will happen when that town finds out we've busted their bridge?"

"Ah! *That* is the reason we're sitting here now. This is a strategy meeting."

Zack studied A. S. Ward carefully. It seemed as though Ward was getting excited. His speech quickened and grew higher-pitched. My God, Zack thought, it's a game to him. "What do you mean, strategy? They'll be mad enough to lynch us."

"True. But they won't." He held up his hand. "Please allow me to finish. They won't because they have no proof. Also, the passengers from the stage will be here as witnesses. Anyone from Running Springs wouldn't dare start trouble. And should someone forget, you gentlemen will see that he's taken care of. After all, it's your town and you have the authority of the law."

"We do?" Bear whispered.

"Of course. And we have a jail. Besides," Ward shrugged. "if they cause a ruckus I will make sure that the stage-line company hears about it. Such a report could only work in our favor."

"Neat," Zack admitted.

Ward shrugged modestly. "Both of you probably thought I was unfair not to help you on the bridge last night. Now I'm sure you appreciate my particular . . . talents. . . . Brains! That, in a nutshell, is my contribution to this partnership."

It was the second insult he'd used since they cracked the bottle. Zack bristled. "In a nutshell! That's a damn good way of putting it, Ward."

The muscles twitched around his eyes. Ward's breath sucked in audibly. The Great Whiskey Palace grew amazingly still. "Mr. Woolsey," Ward gritted, "don't let your pride ruin your future."

"Don't, Mr. Ward, make the mistake of thinkin', because we dress in deerskin duds, that we are stupid."

A trace of amusement played across Ward's mouth. "I'll remember that. Now," he said quickly, "let's talk about the party."

"What party?" Bear asked with sudden interest.

"Why, the party we are going to throw for the stagecoach travelers. You see, we want to show these folks such a fine time that they'll write the Overland Stage Company president absolutely glowing letters about Snakegrass Junction."

"What makes you think they'd do it?" Zack said.

"Wouldn't you, in return for free drinks, lodging, and meals? I'll even write the letters for them if need be. It's really no problem and, again," he emphasized, "excellent promotion."

Zack sipped his whiskey. "That's pretty good," he chuckled appreciatively. "Sure, why not? You don't miss a bit, do you?"

"Never." He hesitated. "Tell me, and I mean no offense, but perhaps I will need some assistance with the letters and—"

"Sorry," Zack said. "Neither of us can read or write."

A. S. Ward smiled disarmingly. "Doesn't matter. I can handle it. You will both be busy enough entertaining."

"Entertaining!" Bear swore. "Who, us?"

"Yes, why not? Most of these passengers will be from the East and have never seen real mountain men like yourselves. Believe me, thanks to the publicity of such men as David Crockett and William Cody, you will be viewed as celebrities."

Bear scratched and fretted. "What sorts of things does celebrities do?"

"Well, perhaps you could stage some small kind of showing. You know, let the people see what you do."

"In towns we just get drunk," Zack said.

"No, no. That won't do. Couldn't you, ahh . . . show them how you bait and set traps, hunt game. Whatever?"

"That's crazy!" Zack spat. "What do we set the traps for around here? Flies and spiders?"

"Think of something else, then. I don't care as long as it's entertainment."

"Well, let me see," Zack said, feeling a rising sense of perversity. "We're both great buffalo skinners. Maybe we could set some traps around the town—ketch us some rabbits and squirrels. Then bring 'em here and skin 'em up slick. What do you say to that?"

"It stinks. Stinks!" Ward scrubbed his face wearily. "Listen, how about just giving them a shooting exhibition? I assume you're good with those cannons you're always holding."

"We could do that, Zack. Couldn't we?"

"I suppose. We could shoot cigars out of their mouths or something."

Ward paled. "No, no. I'll find some targets for you. And no drinking before the exhibition this evening. Deal?"

Zack and Bear emptied their glasses. "Deal," they said in unison.

"Good. Then, gentlemen, I suggest we get started with the preparations. There isn't much time."

Zack rose stiffly from his chair. Hell, he thought, there goes our sleep. But if Ward has misjudged the temperament of Running Springs, we're in for more of a party than he expects.

CHAPTER 9

Darby Buckingham heard the shouting as soon as anyone. He reluctantly put down the copy of a three-week-old New York paper and started for the door. The hollering grew in intensity. From the stores along Main Street, he saw the townspeople standing, then they all seemed to explode into action. Darby hurried after them. It was going to be some kind of trouble. He was sure of it.

Far out on the prairie, he saw two men staggering toward the town. They were hatless and waving and hollering with an amazing amount of vitality, considering their bedraggled appearance.

Darby stopped in his tracks. He didn't have to go a step farther. "The guards," he sighed. He watched the crowd surround the pair. Even though they were almost a half mile away, he could hear the angry shouting. Slowly, Darby turned and walked back to town.

He angled toward the livery barn. He would saddle his horse. Might as well get that over with. Then he'd lead the damn thing over and tie it up in front of his office and wait. It wouldn't take long. Five minutes at most. Then all hell would break loose at his door. The whole town would be demanding action—no, more than action: blood! For they'd know as well as he did that Zack Woolsey and Bear Timberly had struck again. He shuddered to think of what the bridge would look like this time. Probably even worse.

Darby lifted his hands up before his eyes as he trudged along. The blisters were still there. Some had popped and ran with clear fluid. He detested the thought that he'd have to subject them to the same punishment all over again. Damn those two old devils! They'd pushed him and this town far enough.

He saddled in record time. His black gelding didn't even protest when he shoved the bit between its huge yellow teeth. It was just as well, for Darby was in a black mood. Any provocation whatsoever and he would have cracked it between the eyes with his flat, fighter's knuckles.

"Come on," he growled, yanking it outside and down the street to his office.

"Hey, Sheriff! The bridge. It's gone," a man yelled as the crowd surged onto Main Street.

Darby nodded and ducked into his office. He grabbed his shotgun from the gun rack and strode over to the desk. From the top drawer he produced a box of shells. He took a handful and shoved them into his frock coat. He also dropped a derringer in beside them.

Angrily, he broke the breech of the shotgun and loaded it. At that minute, they reached his door. He snapped the shotgun closed viciously and glared at the intruders.

His action seemed to hold them trancelike. Those in front were pushed by those behind. They stared at the gun and then at their sheriff. It was as though they didn't know him. Gone were the soft, easy lines in Darby Buckingham's face. The man who stood before them was formidable. The eyes seemed alive and black as tar. The thick slab of mustache bristled like the hair on a dog's back. There was no welcome in the face. The men being pushed forward into the office resisted and must have wondered what the hell they'd gotten into.

"Where are they?" Darby graveled.

"Who?"

"The guards. I want to talk to them."

"They're at Doc Sawyer's."

Darby walked straight at them and the crowd parted. He saw Dolly Beavers up ahead and strode past her. He was aware that her eyes were wide and fixed on the shotgun. Behind him, he could hear the muffled voices of the crowd as they followed.

When he reached the doctor's office, he went in without knocking. He slammed the door behind him. Doc Sawyer was bent over one man in a chair. The other, the one named Allan, was laying on the examining table. All at once, Darby relaxed and the steel went out of his voice. "How are they, Doctor?"

"They'll be all right," he said, straightening up. The doctor peered at the window. "I see the whole town is gathered out there. I'd say, right at this moment, Darby, you've got more to worry about than my patients. Within five minutes, every citizen in this town who can get a horse will be hunting a rifle and a rope. And there ain't a damn thing you can do about it. Even if Zeb Cather himself could get out of bed, he couldn't change things."

Darby chose not to answer. Instead he went to stand over the second man. "Tell me about it," he demanded.

"There's not much to tell," the guard sighed. "Happened to both of us just about the same way. Last night we got jumped in the dark and that was it. Next thing either of us knew we were staring up at tree limbs and tied tighter than an Indian's drum. I got loose first. Found Al and we hurried back."

"I don't suppose either of you caught a look at who did this?"

"No! But damn it, Sheriff, we all know it was those two crazy hunters."

"How?"

"How! Who else would do it? For what reason? And I'll tell you something else. We ain't got no hearing problems. Nobody could have gotten that close unless they were damn good. Damn good! Unless they were an Indian or a hunter. And if it was Indians, we wouldn't be here now telling you about it."

"But you didn't see them," Darby persisted. "Blast it, anyway! I need proof."

The man's lips curled. "If you do," he hissed, "you're the only one in Running Springs." He tried to get up. Darby pushed him back.

"Where do you think you're going?"

"To find a rope, like everyone else." He grabbed Darby's wrist and started to pull it away.

Darby's fingers collected a wad of the man's shirt front. He drew it up until his back came off the table. "There'll be no hanging," he said softly. "Not by you, or him or anyone. Not as long as I'm your sheriff."

He released the shirt and the man plopped back. "Please. Stay on the table and let the doctor take care of you while I discharge my own responsibilities. Do you understand that?"

The patient nodded rapidly.

"Good." Darby turned back toward the door and placed his hand on the knob. He stood there for a moment to prepare himself. While saddling his horse, he'd realized that his own temper was just as dangerous as those of the townspeople. If he acted in anger, even for a moment, it would all be set into motion. A posse would materialize and everyone would ride toward Snakegrass Junction like a cavalry charge. He didn't want that. He didn't want the inevitable bloodshed to be on his conscience.

So, right there in the barn, he'd decided he would have to set an example and bend their wills to his own. The least sign of weakness or indecision and the game was lost. With or without the law, those people would be swept away with only one thought: vengence.

Darby squared his thick shoulders and opened the door. Right or wrong, he wore the badge and it was going to be handled his way.

They were armed to the teeth and carried enough rope to lasso a Teton mountain. Darby surveyed the mob. His fierce eyes raked their faces. "Go back to your work," he said.

Heads swiveled and the men glanced at one another in disbelief. Then they all pivoted to stare at him.

"We have a posse ready to ride with you," someone called.

"I don't want a posse."

"You what?" A tall young cowboy stepped to the front. "Mister, it don't much matter what you want. As far as I'm concerned, we're just wasting time inviting you to the party. You ain't—"

Darby Buckingham launched himself from the boardwalk. His boots hit dirt at almost the same instant his fist struck flesh. The cowboy slammed back into the crowd, his lips a crimson smear. Two men caught him under the arms and laid him out.

Darby went to his horse, feeling a little guilty. He hadn't wanted to flatten the cowboy. He'd been just a big, overgrown kid trying to impress people. And he hadn't had a chance to even defend himself. What in the devil am I coming to? he thought wearily. He wasn't sure. All he knew was that the kid had stepped into something too big to be toyed with. If he hadn't shut him up very quickly, and with finality, the mob would have caught fire. Darby yanked his reins free from the hitching post and mounted. He made a mental note to look the cowboy up later and offer him an explanation and apology. Perhaps he'd demand a fight to save face. Darby hoped not, because, right or wrong, he knew he'd fight to win.

He started to prod his horse away, but stopped and twisted around in his saddle. His voice, when he spoke, was strong and carried well. "I'm going to ride over to Snakegrass Junction alone," he said. "No one is to follow. You all should be aware that I have no proof to make an arrest."

Surprisingly, it was Mrs. Dooley who stepped up to stand next to his stirrup. "My husband and I have orders that have to be filled in our store. Without that bridge we can't last long in this town." She whirled around, her bustle striking the horse. "None of us can," she charged. There was a rumble of assent from the people. "There," she said, turning back, "you heard them. If you—"

"Don't threaten me, please. I'll do what has to be done. Just like I did when Zeb Cather was shot on this very street and no one dared to track his attackers clear into Nevada."

Her eyes dropped. She was beaten and he felt no pride in the conquest. "Move aside, Mrs. Dooley; I have business." He nudged his horse by her. He could almost smell the hatred. Hatred for reminding them of something everyone wanted to forget.

"Darby! Darby, honey!" It was Dolly. Blast, he thought, not now. "Wait. Please wait!" He pulled his horse up short.

Her fingers gripped his leg. "Why?" she whispered.

He reached down and lifted her chin. "To prevent a massacre," he said. "Dolly, remember how those two told me they were cheated?"

"Yes."

"I believe them and still do. But, without proof, I'm helpless. So, if I was unable to help them because I had no evidence, how could I possibly hurt them without it?"

"But they'll be waiting. Expecting trouble. You'll be riding right into a trap!"

"No," he said, "I don't think so. The man whose calling the shots over there must be this Alvin S. Ward character. The last thing he'll want is to have the sheriff of Running Springs gunned down. He wants that stage line. My death would hardly create a beneficial image."

"Are you sure?" Dolly's eyes told him she wanted to believe his words. Had to believe them.

"Very sure," he said, not feeling sure at all but knowing it sounded good. "I will be back late tonight. Good-by."

"I'll be waiting," she called.

Darby forced his horse into a spine-fracturing gallop. She didn't need to wait up. Thirty-four miles in a saddle would render him insensible. A quivering mass.

He was so shocked at the sight of the destroyed bridge that Darby hardly felt the water when he bullied his horse across the swift Shoshone River. The destruction enraged him all the more when he thought about the long hours he and the citizens of Running Springs had spent rebuilding it. He gained the far bank with only his shotgun and his cigars dry. Darby was mad enough to start smoking—one way or the other. It was a very good thing, he thought, that he'd come alone. If the townspeople had seen the wreckage, he wouldn't have been able to contain them. And in the mood he found himself, he wouldn't have even tried.

Approaching Snakegrass Junction, he was surprised at the size of the town. Coming straight from the East a year earlier, he wouldn't have given it a second glance. But that was a year ago. Since then, he'd seen enough frontier towns to recognize that, once, there had been high optimism in Snakegrass.

Still a good two miles away, he stopped and rechecked the shotgun. He noticed that there were thunderclouds gathering up near the Tetons. The air had a stillness to it, as though everything waited. He took the time to study the land and noticed that Spring had laid a bouquet of small pink and yellow flowers. Darby had a sudden urge to dismount and smell them. Abruptly, he nudged his horse toward the empty buildings. The flowers would have to wait. Perhaps in the weeks to come, he would have Dolly make a picnic and they would come here together. But they'd have to cross the river, and there was no damned bridge. His anger returned.

A mile farther, the thought occurred to him that, ironically, his safety was in the town. For if Zack and Bear chose to suddenly emerge with their long-range hunting rifles, he'd be helpless out here in the open. What was the effective range of a shotgun? Whatever it was, considering his notorious marksmanship he could cut it in half. With this thought, Darby pushed down his derby, gritted his teeth, and whipped the horse into a gallop. In a full out-of-control charge, he entered Snakegrass Junction.

A barrage of gunfire split the street. Darby wildly yanked on the reins. His horse plowed the ground with all four hoofs and he felt himself taking flight. Hang onto the shotgun and roll, he thought. He did. Zeb Cather would have been proud of him. He came still with the shotgun jammed to his shoulder, his eyes straight down the barrel.

Between two buildings, he saw people. A woman turned, saw him, and screamed. People scattered out of sight into the rear alley. Darby relaxed his finger against the trigger. What in—

"Sheriff Buckingham!"

Darby squinted angrily at the two hunters as they hurried toward him. They were smiling. For some reason, that was the last thing he wanted from Zack Woolsey and Bear Timberly.

"What are you doing on your belly?" Zack asked. "You sure don't have to sneak in thataway to join our party."

Darby ignored the proffered hand. He climbed erect, feeling like an idiot. His black suit was caked with dirt and he saw that his derby was crushed and filthy. Must have rolled over it. "I'm not sneaking!" he bellowed.

"Well," Bear replied, "you sure got an unusual way of riding in to visit."

"This is no visit. At least not the kind you'd want. Who are all those people staring at me?"

Zack glanced back. "Don't mind them. They're just the stage passengers. We're putting on a show for 'em back behind the Great Whiskey Palace. They probably think you're part of it."

Darby groaned. "I can't imagine why," he mumbled.

"Let's get off the street. I'm here as a representative of the law. I want to talk to you in private."

"Well, who do we have here?" a man called, striding toward them.

"Alvin S. Ward, I suppose?" Both Zack and Bear nodded. Then, before Darby could speak, the man was pumping his hand like a woman on a butter churn. "Alvin S. Ward, sir. And you must be Darby Buckingham. Yes, yes, of course. I recognize a cultured gentleman when I see one. A writer of note! It's indeed a proud day for my town when—"

"Our town," Zack corrected.

Ward shot Zack as poisonous a look as Darby had ever seen. "As I was saying," Ward continued, "I rarely have the privilege of such distinguished company."

Darby found himself retreating. He couldn't get the man to release his hand. He couldn't take his eyes off the huge gold teeth. Incredible. Four on the top and four on the bottom. Matching sets. Finally, with his free hand, he pried the other's fingers away. "I'm not here for pleasure, sir. I'm here on business. I want to talk with those two."

"Soon, soon. But right now they're beginning to stage a fantastic display of shooting prowess. The passengers have been waiting for this. Would you like to watch?"

"No."

"Then, may I suggest you and I retire to *my*. . . ," he said, emphasizing the word, ". . . to *my* Whiskey Palace. You could dust yourself clean, perhaps wash your face, and then we could have a drink while we wait."

"Confound it," Darby sighed, "what's the use? All right. But then I talk to them. Understand?"

"Perfectly, sir, perfectly." A. S. Ward motioned him toward the saloon. "You are our honored guest."

Darby said nothing but entered the saloon. He stopped. His eyes, accustomed to the outside light, seemed to deceive him. Slowly he walked forward until he was in the center of the floor; then he turned in a full circle, his eyes widening with approval.

"You like it?"

Darby's attention snapped back to Alvin S. Ward. "I am, quite frankly, amazed. This . . . this," he almost failed a description, so great was his surprise, "this is truly an oasis of luxury. Tastefully appointed!"

"Ah, I am pleased you approve. That, sir, was the finest compliment The Great Whiskey Palace has ever received. Such a pity, don't you agree, that it cannot be enjoyed more fully."

Darby grimaced, feeling he'd stepped into a carefully laid trap. He must be cautious; this man was clever. "Not at the expense of Running Springs."

Alvin S. Ward chose not to comment. He passed around behind the elegant bar and produced a bottle. "My best," he explained. "Would you care for a cigar?"

"No, I have my own." He reached into his vest pocket and withdrew a long Cuban. Halfway down, the cigar had snapped. It dangled by its torn wrapper like a broken limb. "Blast," he spat.

"Never mind sir. I'm sure you will find my stock a suitable substitute." With real flourish, Alvin S. Ward produced a wooden box, hand-carved out of what Darby guessed was rosewood.

Darby selected a cigar. "Cuban?" he asked carefully.

"Of course."

"Hmmm. Thank you."

The man lit Darby's cigar, then his own. He poured two generous libations and raised his glass in a toast. "To a rewarding acquaintance, Mr. Buckingham."

Darby said nothing, but tipped his glass and drank. The whiskey was excellent. Almost before his glass touched the bar, it was refilled. Darby smacked his lips reflectively. Was the man going to try to make him drink too much? What for? Darby sipped the whiskey with amusement. This man was too clever for his own good. "What do you mean? Rewarding acquaintance? You and I both know the nature of my business."

"Ah! True. But perhaps there are possibilities you haven't yet considered."

"Such as?"

"This town!" His face changed and Darby saw bitterness etch into the lines of his mouth. "This town was murdered by Running Springs. Murdered! Stabbed in her back and robbed of her very lifeblood."

"The stage, I presume?"

"Yes! The damned stage! But," he said, leaning forward until Darby could smell his breath, "but that will change."

"No," Darby said evenly. "No, it will not. Not if you persist in madness."

Ward reeled back. "Madness," he echoed, shock full in his voice. "What madness?"

"Destroying the bridge."

A laugh burst from between Ward's gold teeth. "I have not destroyed the bridge. Sir, use your eyes! Do I look capable of such an act?"

Darby suppressed an urge to rearrange the gold teeth. He punched his cigar into the corner of his mouth and growled around it. "Of course not. Unless I've misjudged you, you're much to clever to have even gone near the Shoshone River. Instead, ill fate brought you Zack and Bear. They, no doubt, told you of their hatred of Running Springs. And you seized the obvious opportunity."

He poured them another drink. His fingers were steady, Darby noted. Whatever else the man lacked, he had control.

"Of course, Mr. Buckingham, as an officer of the law, I know you must have proof to back this . . . this theory."

He'd been waiting for that. Known it would come. "If I had proof, you and your two friends would be on the way to jail."

"Tsk, tsk. You are in a bad spot, aren't you? I can just imagine what the good citizens of Running Springs are—"

Darby's fist shot out and grabbed him by the shirt front. He yanked Alvin S. Ward halfway up onto the bar. "Don't," he said, "don't be cute with me. I have a very, very short temper. And sometimes, like now, I lose it."

For probably the first time in his life, Ward remained quiet. Darby watched his small eyes plead. The man understood. Darby let him loose and Ward dropped back to the floor. For a moment, neither man spoke.

Then, amazingly, Ward smiled. "My apology," he stammered. Tentatively, he reached out and snatched his drink. This time, Darby noted, the fingers shook badly. Ward tossed his whiskey down and coughed noisily. "I think I've upset you."

"You're a very perceptive man."

"Listen," Ward rushed, "forget what I said. I have a proposition. A good one."

"For who?"

"Both of us! Look, as a famous writer you must have a great many contacts back East."

Darby laughed. "You want me to contact a stage-line official or two. Incredible!"

"That's not it. Do you know any newspaper editors?"

"Of course."

"Good," he sighed. "What I'd like for you to do, Mr. Buckingham, is to write an exclusive account of what is happening here. It's news that would create—"

"Create a great deal of interest in your town."

"Exactly!"

"And what," Darby asked, "if I reported my as yet unproven suspicions?"

Ward blinked. "But that wouldn't be fair! That's not reporting. Just present the facts."

Darby shook his head very slowly. He finished his drink and said, "I find you very amusing. No, Mr. Ward, I will not publicize Snakegrass Junction. I don't know what you had intended to pay me—"

"Everything! I'll give *you* the town. All except this. I would never give up The Great Whiskey Palace."

"Funny. I thought I heard Zack say outside that you'd given the town to them."

"That's crazy," Ward rushed, "why would I give them everything?"

"To destroy the bridge. We've already been over this." He started to walk away.

"Wait!" Alvin Ward rushed around the bar and took a stance by the doorway. "Perhaps I did make certain spurious promises. All right, I admit it."

"That's a start. Now what about the bridge?"

"No!"

"Out of my way."

Ward settled against the doorway. "Listen," he pleaded, "you can have the whole town. I'll settle with those two old men. For a couple of cases of whiskey, they'll be gone tomorrow. We'd never see them again."

Darby's lip curled with distaste. He tore the cigar out of his mouth and hurled it to the floor. He needed fresh air. Fast.

"Believe me, they don't count for anything," Ward called as Darby tramped down the boardwalk.

At the corner of the building, he stopped and took a deep, deep breath. He looked down to see that his fists were knotted so tightly they were white and bloodless. Darby glanced down the alley and saw Bear and Zack surrounded by a crowd. The smell of black powder reminded him that there'd been a shooting exhibit.

The voices were indistinct, because so many people were talking at once. Darby became aware that the crowd was excited. He turned his thoughts from Alvin S. Ward and watched with fascination. He saw Bear and Zack finish loading and take their stances together. The crowd grew quiet.

A young man in a brown suit detached himself from the others and, shoulders squared, walked jauntily out toward the prairie. He traveled a long ways and only stopped when Zack called, "Far enough."

Unable to resist the impulse, Darby hurried down the alley for a closer look. He saw the young man bend down and pluck two small pink flowers. Then, very dramatically, he lifted both arms straight out from his sides. The flowers sprouted from each hand, poised between thumb and forefinger. His voice reached them, surprisingly loud and strong. "Whenever you are ready, Mr. Woolsey, Mr. Timberly."

Darby felt his heart quicken as the two hunters raised their rifles to their shoulders. And then, without seeming to take aim, there were black smoke and thunder. Flowers vanished. The onlookers cheered and Darby had to smile when the young man lost his composure and let out a wild whoop.

He could see the two hunters grinning and chuckling as the stage passengers congratulated them. It amused him to see that there was something of the ham in both men. Probably the first time in their lives they'd received that kind of attention from their fellow man. Let them have their moment, he thought, but then he'd have his say.

"Shooting is over," Zack proclaimed. "Now it's time for drinking and dancing. Bear, here, is going to do a Kiowa rain dance on the bar. Drinks on the house!"

Another cheer went up. The passengers filed toward the saloon and Darby angled over to intercept Bear and Zack. "Quite a show," he said.

Zack winked slyly. "You won't see none better."

"Ah, but I have."

"Who?" Bear demanded.

"To tell the truth, I don't know. But not long ago someone shot a cigar out of my mouth on the Shoshone Bridge."

Bear and Zack glanced at each other and began to wheeze with suppressed laughter.

"It's not funny," Darby said. "If I find out who did it, I'll make sure it never happens again."

"Oh," Zack chuckled, "you just do that, Sheriff."

"Another thing. If I can find proof that you two are responsible for destroying the bridge, you'll go to jail."

The laughter disappeared. Zack twisted sideways and spat into the dirt. When he turned back, his voice was hard. "You try that, Mister Writer Man, and we'll see you planted."

"Maybe," Darby replied. "But you've been warned."

"And so have you," Bear said.

Darby walked over to his horse and mounted. He reined around to find them watching him. "You should know that your partner just tried to sell you out for a couple of cases of whiskey. That's what he thinks you're worth."

"He's got a lot to learn," Zack growled. "And so do you."

Darby nodded. "I'll give you one more thing to think about, gentlemen. The people in Running Springs wanted to hang all of you when I left. We'll be rebuilding the bridge starting tomorrow. If anything happens to it again, proof or no proof, I'm coming over after you."

"Your funeral, Sheriff. The only thing that might make things square between us and you is that six hundred dollars we was cheated outa!"

"What if I gave you the money?" Darby asked suddenly.

"Why?"

"Because I'd rather do that than have you in my jail or have to shoot you."

The two men looked at each other in astonishment. Zack pulled off his hat and scratched his head. "City man, I give you credit," he said. "You've got stomach."

"The offer. Will you accept?"

"Can't. We wouldn't take your money, 'cause that would mean that gambler would come out ahead. He's the one that has to pay. Not you."

"That's what I was afraid you'd say. Then, that's it."

He rode out of Snakegrass Junction without looking back. It was too bad, Darby thought. As nearly as he could figure it, there was only one possible solution: Edward Hyder.

Darby splashed into the river and swam his horse across just as the sun went down. There wasn't much time. Somehow, he'd have to trap the gambler and find proof. But how?

Maybe, he thought, it was time to have a talk with Zeb Cather.

CHAPTER 10

"Well," Zeb drawled, "it sounds like you're in a real fix. Are you sure that this Woolsey and Timberly were cheated?"

Darby Buckingham frowned. "No. Not completely. But I've questioned the bartender at the Concord and he says that Edward Hyder is as slick a gambler as he's seen in a long time."

"You should have run him out of town," Zeb said.

"Run him out! Why, I've gone to a great deal of trouble to keep him here. If that man leaves with Zack and Bear's six hundred dollars, I'll never be able to resolve the problem in Snakegrass Junction without killing."

Zeb Cather hitched himself up higher onto his pillow. "If it was me, I'd arrest those two old buffaloers and toss them in jail along with Hyder." He smiled. "I guarantee you'd get to the truth in mighty quick time."

"They'd kill him in a minute."

"Well, maybe you'd hear his dying confession. Maybe he'd talk before he'd go into a cell with them."

"That's not a legal confession."

"Look, Darby. I know the law better'n you. And I'd agree that no lawyer would approve of the method. But it would work. Unless I miss my bet, that gambler would be so scared he'd talk a blue streak. He'd produce that marked deck faster than I could drop a gun hammer."

Darby lapsed into a brooding silence. The sheriff's solution was direct, and simple. If he were Zeb Cather, he'd probably do it that way. But what the old lawman failed to realize was that Darby wouldn't be able to pull it off. The reasons were obvious, and Darby mentally ticked them off. One, he wasn't adept enough with a gun to get the drop on Zack and Bear. So, two, he'd have to kill them before they'd submit to a jail cell. Three. Even if, somehow, he did manage to bring them back alive, they'd be so furious they'd probably tear the bars out of the window. Darby knew Bear's strength was nearly a match for his own. Cather's jail wouldn't last a night. Finally, number four, he had no proof to arrest Edward Hyder. The gambler knew that as well as he knew Bear and Zack would kill him instantly. The gambler was too shrewd to fall for the scheme.

What it all boiled down to, then, was that Zeb Cather might be able to pull it off, but he, Darby Buckingham, couldn't. Zeb Cather wouldn't be able to understand these things. He was a straightforward lawman who'd gained a lifetime of experience dealing with the basic problem of kill or be killed.

Darby rose to his feet. "I'll think about it," he said.

"You already have and you won't do it." Zeb's lined face relaxed into a smile. "Sit down, Buckingham. I'm the reason you're faced with this mess. So I reckon before you leave we'll figure something you and I can agree on. Now, I've told you what *I'd* do. What do *you* want to try?"

Darby eased back into the chair. "Well, my plan would be to set this Hyder up and catch him cheating."

"But you told me he's playing it cagey. All he wants to do is lay low until the doctor removes that thing around his neck, then take the next stage out. If he's as smart as you think, he'll never take your bait."

"If he's an inveterate cheat, he won't be able to resist. The temptation must be too great to pass up."

"How much temptation are you thinking of, Darby?"

"A thousand dollars ought to do it."

A low whistle escaped from Zeb Cather's lips. "Where in the deuce are you going to get that kind of money?"

Darby waved the question aside. "My New York publisher, Mr. J. Franklin Warner, will be more than happy to advance me a line of credit at the bank. A simple telegraph will do it."

"Huh," Cather grunted. "Sometimes I forget that you're not one of us. But, even so, it's risky. What if it turns out that Hyder doesn't cheat? He may very well end up with all your money and you'll be left hanging."

"All right," Darby said. "Though I won't be able to face him across the poker table personally, I'll still be placing my bet. Besides, I feel certain it will work."

"Sure oughta. Hell, I'd be tempted to cheat, myself, to win a thousand dollars! That's more than I make in a year."

"The next thing we have to decide, Zeb, is who can I trust to play against Hyder? Whoever it is would certainly be facing danger. When I step in to make an arrest, there's an outside chance Hyder will panic and shoot."

"Hell, yes!" Zeb swore. "He'd stand to lose at least sixteen hundred dollars."

"So the man we get will be taking a risk, and he'll have to be enough of an actor to play both drunk and foolish. But convincingly."

"I got just the one for you."

"Who?"

"Andy Carson," Cather said. "Why, he was just by here yesterday. Said he'd told the stage company he wouldn't drive his coach into Snakegrass Junction, no matter what. They told him as long as the bridge was out he'd do it or he was out of a job. So he quit."

"That's it, then. He has every reason to help us get this mess resolved."

"And he's been drunk enough to play the part. Even more important, Andy Carson ain't scared of anything."

"I'll go find him," Darby said, jumping up and starting for the door.

"Hey, Buckingham."

Darby turned.

"Still seems almighty complicated. My way is better."

"Probably," he admitted. "But you just stay in bed and get well. The moment you are strong enough to carry around this badge is the moment I'll once again become a contented man."

Darby closed the door on Cather's laughter. He had one thought in mind, and that was to find Andy Carson. On the last leg of his journey from the East, he'd had occasion to do a few favors for the crotchety old stage driver. Perhaps Andy would remember.

Andy Carson sat on the top rail of the corral and chewed reflectively on his tobacco. Darby had found him brooding, watching the horses and spitting at imaginary targets in the dust. "So you say if we trap this Hyder fella and you return the money to those mean old farts in Snakegrass Junction, everything will be the way it used to be."

"Yes."

"And what if they don't want the money back? That Alvin S. Ward is a smooth-tongued son of a bitch and he's probably convinced them they're going to be rich."

Darby swallowed. He hadn't even considered the thought. He didn't want to now. Everything he'd planned was based on the assumption that, once Bear and Zack had their six hundred dollars returned, they'd end the vendetta and ride off to do whatever they did. What Andy Carson had just suggested wasn't possible.

"Well?" Andy interrupted. "You ain't answered my question."

"They'll leave. They don't belong in a town. You know that as well as I do."

"Sure but do they?" Andy spit a streak of tobacco and nailed a red ant at seven feet. "I've seen it happen before. Every time some idiot yells, 'Gold strike,' people who've generally acted normal all their lives suddenly go crazy. Heard of one stagecoach driver who passed a rider on his way to town from the mountains. All the rider did was yell, "Gold!" and the goddamn stagecoach driver headed for the strike, passenger, baggage, and all."

"We're not talking about gold."

"Same thing, Sheriff. Only, instead of gold, it's owning a whole town. Maybe even worse."

Darby drew out a cigar and stuffed it into his mouth. He didn't like the way the conversation was going. What especially irritated him was that there might be more to Andy Carson's line of reasoning than he dared to admit. He struck a match against the fence post and puffed rapidly. "Look, Andy. I can't promise anything for sure. All I want to know is, will you do it?"

"Well, well, I guess it would be more fun than sitting up here chewing. Yeah! OK, I'm in as long as it's your money— and your whiskey I'm drinking."

"Good!" Darby took a deep breath of relief. "I'll have your stakes today. Come up to my room this evening and I'll explain it all to you there."

Andy Carson returned his attention to the corral and the horses. "That big black of yours looks strong enough to carry five men your size. He moves good, too."

"Looks are deceiving, Mr. Carson. See you tonight."

Darby stopped in the alley. "Well, this is it," he said. "Here's the money. You know what to do. I'll be in the back room very close. Make sure the cards are marked before you call. Then I'll come in and make my arrest."

"Don't you worry none. If he's cheating, ol' Andy will nail him." He lifted a bottle of whiskey and Darby saw it slosh against the moonlight. "I hate a cheat. I'll get him for you."

"No! That's exactly what I don't want. Are you armed?"

Andy Carson glared at him strangely. "Damn right. Fool question."

"Give me your gun."

"What? You're crazy! I'd sooner walk in there naked."

"Just the same," Darby persisted. "I must insist. The gun."

Carson grumbled, but produced a navy Colt from his waistband. "Anything else?"

"No. Just good luck. And thanks."

"Say," he said, "if I win, can I keep it?"

"Of course."

"That's good. I would have anyway."

When Andy Carson reached the end of the alley at Main Street, Darby saw him pull the bottle out of his coat pocket and take a long drink. Then the driver disappeared around the corner toward the Concord Saloon. Darby shook his head doubtfully. He wasn't at all sure Andy Carson could pull it off. If the man was intoxicated or a poor poker player, perhaps Edward Hyder wouldn't even need to use a marked deck. Then, what was to be done? About all he could do would be to wait in the back room until Andy lost the entire one thousand dollars. To break in on the game would ruin any chances of ever trapping the gambler. Hyder was smart. He'd be out on the next stage no matter what Dr. Sawyer told him.

Darby lit a cigar and smoked. He wanted to give Andy plenty of time to set the game up. Earlier, in Darby's room, they'd both agreed it would have to be Hyder who initiated the play. All Andy had to do was make sure the gambler saw the size of his bankroll. They'd even hit upon an explanation for Andy to use concerning how he happened to have so much money. Since everyone in town knew he'd quit the stage line after more than ten years of driving, he'd just say it was from back wages and savings. Hyder would believe that, and so would anyone else.

He forced himself to smoke slowly. The cigar seemed to last forever. But, finally, he dropped it to the earth and rubbed it out with his heel. Then he headed for the back door.

Besides himself, Zeb Cather, and Andy Carson, they'd had to let one more person in on this plan. Carl was on duty, and just as promised, he'd left the back door unlocked.

In his novels, Darby had several times described the secret back room of a saloon. It was supposed to be luxurious, fit only for the high-stakes players, the select few. In the case of the Concord Saloon, he was disappointed to discover the back room to be no more than a storage area. Oh, to be sure, it held its delights. Case after case of cheap whiskey piled almost to the ceiling. There were also tangles of broken tables and chairs, cobwebbed and dusty.

All these things Darby saw at a glance. He purposefully left the rear door open to give a small measure of light. Then, on tiptoes, he carefully advanced toward the door that led into the main saloon. The sounds of laughter and talk blended as they reached his ears. Darby crouched by the door and listened.

It was impossible. The voices he heard were indistinct, a constant rumbling punctuated now and then by a loud outburst of laughter. He placed his ear next to the wood, strained to distinguish the voice of Andy Carson or Hyder. For almost a full minute, he leaned against the door. Suddenly, it slammed him roughly and he heard a loud crash inches away. Darby grabbed his ear and massaged it painfully.

"Guess I've had too much to drink," he heard Andy shout. The door rattled again and Darby heard Andy slide up the wood. "I won't be playing long."

"You can quit whenever you want." Darby's pulse quickened. It was Hyder. He heard the sounds of chairs scrape, then, "Deal."

As near as Darby could tell, Andy won the first two hands. But, on the third, Hyder raised the bet and won a hundred dollars. The gambler lost one more, for twenty-six dollars, betting against two pair.

"Let's play for some real money. How about it, old timer?"

"That's what I'm here for. How about setting the ante at twenty-five dollars a hand?"

Not too fast, Darby thought. Not too fast.

"Suits me. I believe it's my deal."

From what Darby could tell, the game began to change rapidly. Edward Hyder started to win big. Andy Carson wasn't talking much any more. Just grunts and an occasional curse. Darby found himself paying particular attention to who dealt when Hyder won. He was not surprised, in the course of the next hour, to find that Hyder won almost every hand he dealt. But something was wrong. He was also winning when Andy dealt! Darby began to sweat. More than once, he heard Hyder say in almost an embarrassed tone, "Guess it's just my lucky night."

Luck, hell, Darby thought. It's got to be that deck! He drew out Andy Carson's gun and laid it across his knee.

"Bartender, bring another bottle over here!"

Darby rubbed his face nervously. Why didn't Carson signal him!

Next he heard Carl set the bottle down loudly. "Don't you think you've had enough, Andy?"

"Let him alone, goddammit!" Hyder snapped.

Andy's voice sounded slurred. "I gotta take a walk. Be right back. Then we'll play one more hand. Winner take 'er all." He burped. "You wanna do that?"

There was no hesitation at all in the reply. "I'd be less than a sport to deny you the chance to recoup. I'll be waiting."

Darby heard a key scratch in the door. He leapt back just as it opened and heard Carl say, "Go through the back way. It's faster."

Andy Carson stumbled into the room and wobbled out into the alley. Darby glanced at the door into the saloon. It was only partially cracked. Without hesitation, Darby hurried out into the alley.

"Thunder and blast!" he swore, grabbing Carson by the coat and spinning him around. "Why didn't you signal me?" he rasped. "You're getting drunk and losing my money!"

"No, I ain't." The man fumbled his pants together and turned around. "In fact, I had Carl mix me a couple of bottles of tea this afternoon with no more than a shot of whiskey in either one of 'em."

"What?"

"That's right." Carson grimaced with obvious distaste. "Terrible concoction."

Darby's hands dropped to his side. "But why didn't you signal?"

"Because he isn't using a marked deck."

"What!" Darby's eyes bulged in disbelief.

"Dammit, it's not marked."

"But . . . but all the money you've lost."

"Can't help it. I never was much good at poker. And I'll tell you something, Sheriff. That feller in there is so good he don't need to cheat."

Darby groaned. He clenched both fists and raised them to the sky in supplication. "How stupid can I be?"

"Take it easy. We still got a chance."

"How? For God's sake, man, give me some hope."

"One more hand. That's what I told him. Winner take all."

"So?"

"So, one hand by itself can go to whoever has luck. Over the long run the best player wins. But on one hand you got to be lucky. No matter how good you are, a fistful of nothing gets you nothing."

"Do you mean Hyder will have to cheat?"

"Hell, yes! What else? Right now, he's alone, so he could switch decks. And I made sure it's his deal."

"Brilliant! Absolutely brilliant!" Darby rushed. "With all that money riding on one single hand he can't possibly take a chance of losing." He grasped Andy Carson by the shoulders and shook him until the older man's head snapped back and forth. "I apologize!"

"I accept. Lemme loose!" Carson broke free, his eyes huge. He swallowed. "I better get back before he gets suspicious."

Andy tottered into the back room and on out to the saloon. He shut the door behind him with a click. Darby was inside instantly, his ear pressed against the wood and the gun in his hand.

"How many cards?"

"Three."

"Ah, dealer takes one."

"No, you're wrong. The dealer just takes a trip to jail."

Darby heard chairs scrape, then a shout. He'd waited too long. He surged against the door with all his strength, and wood splintered. The door crashed inward, and Darby saw Edward Hyder spin, with a leveled gun, away from Carson. A bullet bit into the door. Then another splintered wood by his face. Darby brought his weapon up and began firing. He was no more than ten feet from Edward Hyder—and he couldn't miss. The gambler took two shots squarely. He slammed back into the rear wall, his own gun coughing bullets at the floor. "You . . . you set me up," he gasped. "You cheated me!" Then he died.

Darby dropped the door. Without even being aware of it, he'd held it up by the knob. It had saved his life. "Andy, are you all right!"

"Yeah. Just fine. Carl," Andy hollered, "bring me a bottle of the real stuff." He turned back to Darby. "You won't believe this, but he had me cold. Know why he didn't shoot?"

"No."

"Because he was waiting for me to draw first, so it would be self-defense. He was as cool as ice. He was going to give me all the time I needed. If I'd have had my gun, I'd have gone for it and the gambler would have ventilated me. I don't know how to tell you this, but I could tell by the look on his face he'd been through it all before."

Darby nodded. He stepped over and peered down at the body. "Did you hear him? He called me a cheat. I never thought of it that way—but he did. I didn't want to kill him."

"You had no choice. Besides, he opened up first. I saw both his bullets take hunks outa the door. You were sure goddamn slow—and lucky."

"I guess I was," Darby whispered. He knelt down and selected several face cards. Without a word, he stood up and walked under a lamp. Very deliberately he studied them. When he looked up at Carl and Andy there was almost a smile on his face. "They're marked," he said. "Just like Zack Woolsey said they'd be. "They're marked!"

Carl shoved a glass of whiskey into his hand. "Have a chair, Mr. Buckingham. You look like a man who needs to take a load off. Please, sir, have a drink."

Before the evening was over, almost the entire adult population of Running Springs had passed through the Concord Saloon. But they didn't find their sheriff, Darby Buckingham, for he was out on the prairie with Dolly Beavers.

They walked hand in hand under a pale, glowing moon. The night was almost dead still. Only the occasional yip-yip of a coyote sounded. The night was soothing and peaceful.

Darby took a deep breath. "You know, I'd much prefer writing about gunfights than being involved in them."

"Of course," she said. "It's not your calling to be violent."

"Sometimes I wonder about that, myself. When I was a boy I was taught to fight. I carried it with me into manhood. When I fought professionally all those years, it was only toward the end that I realized I loved it."

"How can you say that?"

—

"Because it's true." Darby nudged a small clump of grass with the toe of his shoe. When it resisted, he kicked it free. "I don't think, I really don't believe I enjoy hurting things or people. The best way I can figure it is that I enjoy the contest, and the danger. When I was waiting in the back room of the Concord Saloon tonight, I felt. . . ." He paused, searching for the right word. "I felt exhilarated by the prospect of danger. Is that crazy?"

"Not crazy, just strange."

"No, be serious!"

"I am. Listen," she said, moving very close and studying his face. "I can't give you any answers. You're the one who has seen so much of life, not me. All I can try to do is understand how you feel. But I'll say this. I've met hundreds of men who loved danger. Most of them died for it."

Darby smiled. "Yes, I suppose it is a rather perilous addiction."

"Particularly when you can't shoot straight."

"I was accurate enough tonight."

"You were very fortunate. But what about tomorrow?"

"Tomorrow it will all work out. I'll ride over to Snakegrass Junction and return Zack and Bear their six hundred dollars. They'll disappear into the sunset and, once we repair the bridge, life will return to normal around here."

"What if they won't leave? What will you do then?"

"I don't know," he admitted. "I'll just handle the question when it becomes necessary."

Dolly shivered. "I'm getting cold; can we go back?"

"Of course, my dear. I think I know just what we need."

"Of course," she laughed.

CHAPTER 11

In direct violation of his nature, Darby Buckingham rose very early the next morning. He dry-shaved by lamplight, nicking himself several times in his haste. He dressed in his usual attire, white shirt, black tie and suit, and derby hat. It was easier that way, always dressing the same. Over the years, he'd found that decisions made early in the morning were usually faulty anyway. So he'd simply eliminated the choice of what to wear. The only deviation he permitted this morning was to substitute, for his usual, round-toed shoes, a pair of high-heeled western boots.

He reached into his dresser and produced a derringer. He expected no trouble but wanted to be prepared. The gunfight and killing of Edward Hyder the night before was still much on his mind. Darby also collected six hundred dollars and slipped it into his inside coat pocket.

Outside, the beginning of day streaked the eastern sky. Darby hurried toward the livery stable. He intended to depart before the town awakened.

The barn was pitch black inside, but he found a bridle and snatched a handful of hay from a stack. The horse wouldn't come unless bribed. Darby came to the corral and peered through the rails. The black gelding was standing in among its friends. Darby stepped between the rails and waved the hay enticingly. The only problem with this gambit was that all the horses came running.

Darby edged back against the fence and braced himself for the onslaught. There was a flashing of mottled yellow teeth, and Darby jumped. His arm encircled the gelding's neck and the horse reared. Darby shoved the cold, steel bit at its mouth and heard it strike teeth. The gelding snorted and back-pedaled, but he still managed to force the device into its mouth. There! It was done. Once the horse knew the bit was between his teeth, the fight went out of him. Darby slipped the bridle over the animal's head, flattening the ears in the process. Then he started for the gate.

Back inside the barn, he led the horse to the stack of hay and hunted until he found his blankets and saddle. The animal gulped down the hay with great enthusiasm. It always amazed Darby how a horse could eat and swallow with the bit in its mouth. As far as he was concerned, it was their greatest accomplishment. He saddled and rode out. This is it, he thought; in a few hours the whole mess will be resolved—I hope.

He forded the river and set his horse to a gallop. There was really no hurry, but he hadn't slept well all night, thinking about Zack and Bear. If they took the money and departed Snakegrass Junction, Darby knew, his problems were over. One thing was very evident: without the two old hunters, Alvin S. Ward posed little threat. The man would have no choice but to abandon his grandiose scheme.

To Darby's way of thinking, Ward was fairly repre-sentative of a type that the West attracted too often: the for-tune seeker. Somehow, the man must have made a financial killing and used the proceeds to build his saloon. Darby had to credit him with taste: The Great Whiskey Palace was the finest drinking establishment he'd seen west of the Mississippi River. Too bad it would fall into decay when abandoned, he thought, seeing it in the distance.

The gelding was beginning to blow hard. Darby pulled it in and relaxed at a walk. It was a beautiful morning. He hoped it would stay that way. It would all depend on Bear and Zack.

If it was at all possible, he decided, he would talk to the two hunters in private. It didn't take a great deal of intelligence to predict Ward's reaction. The man would try every trick at his disposal to keep Bear and Zack in town. Darby didn't underestimate his persuasiveness.

So, he reasoned, if I can get the two of them to myself, I'll have a better chance of convincing them to leave. And if worse came to worst, he would get tough. After all, he'd returned their money, and any grudge they might have with Running Springs was over. He, as sheriff, had killed a man and risked the life of another trying to get proof. Zack and Bear could expect no more. "A fair return," Darby said aloud, entering the main street. "I've done my part."

He saw them in a great cloud of dust. Darby reined in the gelding and stared at the open door of the hotel. He saw shadows moving as the dust rolled out the doorway. There was loud coughing, and suddenly, Bear and Zack stumbled out to lean on the porch posts. "I see you gentlemen are doing a little house cleaning," he called.

They snapped around. Darby saw sheepishness replace surprise. Zack cleared his breath. "It's woman's work." He swore. "But it has to be done before the stage arrives this afternoon."

"That's right," Darby said. "Today is Thursday. Are you going to do your amazing feats of marksmanship?"

"Sure. That why you're here? To watch?"

"Not exactly. I have some good news for you."

"I doubt it, Buckingham." Zack seemed to weigh a decision but at last said, "We got some coffee brewed inside. Guess I could spare some, if you ain't here wanting trouble."

"It would go well," Darby said. "I left Running Springs very early, and I come in peace."

"I'll get it for us," Bear said. He bulled into the hotel and Darby could hear him coughing again. He didn't have the nerve to ask if the coffeepot was covered. He'd find out soon enough anyway.

Darby unloaded himself from his saddle and tied the horse at a nearby rail. He approached the tall man and they both squatted down to wait for Bear.

"Man, I tell you," Zack said quietly, "me and Bear been working like slaves since we owned this town. And we ain't even scratched the surface yet! I'm beginning to understand why Ward let us have the place. It's too much work."

"I can imagine."

"I doubt it. Me and Bear couldn't when we started. Everything looked just dandy to us. But, you stick around long enough, and just sit and watch, you begin to see all the things need fixin'. Hell, last night the three of us were just standing here and a board fell off the wall yonder. Just dropped in the street!"

"Must have been awful."

"It was! You can't understand the pressure until you own a town." He took a deep breath and sighed. "And to think we used to talk about how hard skinning buffalo was all day. Hell, keeping the boards tacked up is only one part of the fixin' up."

"There's more, eh?"

"Yeah. Lots. For instance, Ward pointed out how all these buildings oughta be painted. And you know what?"

"What?"

"He's right. Buckingham, I laid in bed last night and I swear I could hear the damn paint cracking clear up and down the street. I tell ya, it's hard."

"Then, why do it? Seems you and Bear have survived all these years without a town."

Zack chuckled. "Hell, you're spittin' in the rain. I know what you want. You'd like Bear and me to give up on this and clear out. It would make all those folks in Running Springs happy."

"Yes, but—"

"Forget it," Zack growled. "We're going to have us a nice

friendly cup of coffee. Then you can ride back the way you come. No hard feelings."

Bear emerged carrying three mugs and a pot. He set them down on the boardwalk and poured. Darby eyed his cup thoughtfully. He let Bear and Zack drink first.

"Ah," Bear said smacking his lips. "Always better the second week."

"For a fact," Zack sipped.

"Cigar?" Darby offered.

"Would you look at those things, Bear?"

Bear did more than look, he snatched them. They all lit up and sat smoking. Darby felt uneasy. He didn't like the way Zack had spoken. At first, when the man had started complaining about the upkeep, Darby had let him go on. It had seemed as though it was going to go in the proper direction. But, somehow, it hadn't.

"I said I had some good news for you," he began.

"Let me guess," Zack said. "That good-lookin' Dolly Beavers is pining away to see us."

They both laughed heartily. Darby chewed his cigar and waited until they stopped. "Not exactly. Here is your six hundred dollars," he said, reaching into his pocket and extracting the wad of bills from his wallet. He held it out until Zack slowly took the money.

The laughter was gone. "How'd you come by this?"

Darby told them the story and they listened in silence. When he was finished, he presented two marked cards for their inspection. "That's proof, gentlemen. I'm just sorry I couldn't have gotten it a lot sooner. Your destroying the bridge twice has caused Running Springs a great deal of work and lost business."

"Wait there just a minute," Zack said. "You ain't got no proof it was us."

Darby slammed his cup down so hard coffee shot into the air. "Proof! Listen, you two, since the first time I set eyes on you my life has been plagued with trouble. Now, I've given you back your money and that's the end of it. I want you to saddle up your horses and leave this place."

"And if we don't?"

"I've got a town of people who have all the proof they need to hang you. If you decide to stay, I won't be responsible for them."

"You'd better be." Darby turned and saw Alvin S. Ward standing in the street. "You're the sheriff and you have a duty to protect us."

"Wrong. My duty is to the people of Running Springs."

"Same thing. If they come riding over here to lynch us, some of them aren't going to leave."

Darby stood up, his eyes smoldering. He glared at Ward. "You really think you can pull this one off, don't you?"

"I'm sure of it," Ward replied. "I've got a stack of letters from Tuesday's passengers to the president of the stage company. By tomorrow, I'll have more. You can believe me when I say Running Springs is dead. And you can tell those folks we have a town that needs citizens—provided they're willing to pay the rent."

"I'm sure you'll be very generous with your terms."

"Of course. Bear, Zack, and I have already set the prices. They are attractive, considering everything is already in place. Naturally," he smiled, "those that come first will realize the most favorable terms."

Darby snapped around to face Bear and Zack. "I'll spell out my terms to you. The bridge will be fixed before the month is over. I'll ride back this morning and go out with a work party this afternoon. We won't roll over and die. And when the bridge is finished, I'll recruit an army to guard it if necessary."

"Might be," Zack said.

"What?"

"An army might be necessary."

"No, it won't. And I'll tell you why. If it happens again, I'll lead a posse over here. Proof or no proof, we'll run you out and burn this place to the ground."

Zack and Bear climbed to their feet and Darby raised his fists. "Come on," he whispered. "This time, things will be different."

"Hold it!" Alvin S. Ward jumped between them.

"Bear, Zack, don't you see? He wants to provoke us. What has he got to lose?"

"His head," Bear spat.

"No! It's us that will lose. He's scared 'cause he knows we'll win. The letters! I tell you we've whipped Running Springs!"

Darby whirled for his horse. It was no good talking to them. Alvin S. Ward had them spellbound with his slippery words. Darby tore the reins from the hitching rail and climbed into the saddle. He ignored Ward; the man was beyond belief.

He looked at Zack and Bear. "I thought we had an understanding."

"The only understanding we have, Buckingham, is that we are bettin' each other will lose." Zack's voice dropped. "You did what you said you'd do about that gambler. Bear and me are obliged to you for that. We'll use the six hundred to buy paint and fix-up for this place. 'Cause we're staying."

"You're wrong," Darby replied, "and I think you know it. You've listened to a crazy fraud and he led you into his own madness. I've given you back your money and, if you ride away now, you will be no worse off than the first day we met."

"Yes we would. Bear and me have got something here that is worth more than all of us. A town. Our town! Up to now we never had nothing ahead but hardship and an unmarked grave. Things are different now. You saw those passengers. How they cheered for us. We're something now. Not just two old men fighting to survive one more winter. Growing stiffer by the season."

"It didn't have—"

"I ain't through. You can't understand what this chance means to Bear and me. Hell, why should you? You're a writer! Got money, people looking up their noses, and a suit to wear so folks don't forget their places. Except for this town, we ain't got nothing."

"You're alive," Darby said. "And you've got six hundred dollars that you earned in honest work."

"Six hundred dollars wouldn't do much more than stock us for another season and keep our bellies full next year. It ain't enough. Do you understand me, it ain't goddamn near enough!"

Darby shook his head in defeat. "I understand." For almost a minute there was silence. Zack and Bear studied the ground as if they were ashamed. Maybe, Darby thought, the man had said more than he'd intended. Said it with desperation, and from his heart. Even Ward was quiet and subdued. Darby cleared his throat. "All I know is that you're hurting a lot of good people like Dolly Beavers. I can't let you keep doing it."

Zack's head came up straight. He looked Darby in the eye. "Tell Dolly and the others we wish it didn't have to be that way. Tell 'em it don't. They cross the river and join us, they'll be treated like brethren. We'll have a better town than Running Springs ever thought to be. Tell them, in time they'll thank us."

"I can't tell them that, Zack. They wouldn't listen."

"Then, we'll tell them!'

"What do you mean, Zack?" Bear asked.

"Just what I said, by damn! We'll ride over and extend a personal invite to all who'll listen."

Darby groaned.

"Don't fret, city man, we'll come in peace. Won't even bring our rifles. No trouble this time."

"No trouble!" Darby exploded. "You two are the personification of trouble."

"Aw, well, maybe we have been a little wild in the past. But we've changed. Want everyone to know it. We're businessmen now." Unexpectedly, Zack smiled and glanced at his partner. "Shall we warn him?"

"About what?"

"You know." Zack swept an arm from chin to shin.

"Oh, yeah. Sure."

There was a definite hint of bedevilment in Zack's eyes. "Well, we were talking about it after you rode out the other day. And Ward agreed. If we're going to be respectable town owners, we got to look the part. So . . . so we ordered suits just like you're wearing."

Darby blinked. Involuntarily, he glanced down at his own clothes. "Like this!"

"That's right. Ward measured us up and sent the order off with the stage."

"You," Darby hissed, "You did that?"

Ward swallowed noisily, then nodded.

"You are even lower than I'd thought."

"I—"

"Shut up," Darby roared, "or I'll climb down and thrash you where you stand."

"What's wrong with him?" Bear asked.

"Beats me," Zack said. "Thought he'd take it proud."

"Suit or no suit, if you come to Running Springs, there'll be trouble. I advise you against it."

"When are you going to get it through your head, Buckingham, Bear and me don't like advice?"

Darby reined the gelding away. He rode out of town and didn't glance back. They'd been warned. He could do no more.

"Tell Dolly we'll be in to see her," came a shout.

Darby's mustache bristled but he kept going.

CHAPTER 12

Darby raised his hand in signal. He bent over until his chest touched the water and, as the two ropes tightened on the log, he set his feet in the mud and heaved. For a moment, the log stayed, wedged tightly as it was among others. Then, almost easily, it began to move. Darby strained until the muscles in his shoulders and arms corded and quivered. The log gave a mud-sucking sound and rose. Darby's chest came out of the river and the log began to turn with the current.

The ropes went slack. He reached over and pulled them loose, scraping knuckles against bark. The log shifted farther into the river, suddenly caught the main current, and began to bob away. Darby waved tiredly to the horsemen above and sloshed over to the bank. He sat down heavily.

It was the fourth day. Tomorrow the river would be clear and they could begin to cut new logs. Four days, he thought, of punishment.

At first they'd argued whether to move the bridge a few hundred feet upstream. Just leave the tangled logs alone and start from scratch. Darby himself had been for it, because he knew clearing the logs would be dangerous work. But Andy Carson changed their minds. He'd pointed out that the pilings in the center of the river were still solid. They'd been set eight years earlier and he'd helped do it. Fall was the only time to place them, when the water was at its lowest point. Great holes had to be dredged so the pilings went deep. That, he argued, was the bridge's strength. The pilings were buried and back-filled with boulders. As nearly as Andy could remember, it had taken them almost two weeks—just on the pilings.

So they'd cursed, and started breaking loose the fallen timbers. The first day had been the worst. The logs were so jammed they hadn't known where to start. The most obvious place was on the downstream side along the edges. Trouble was, if a man were in the water, the whole thing might break loose and pull him under. It took Darby almost a whole morning to decide that there wasn't any choice. So he and those others without family had climbed out onto the logs and started to work. Now it was almost over. Only four timbers remained. They were wrapped around the middle pilings. They were going to be hard to dislodge, hard even to reach.

Andy Carson squatted down beside him. "Goddamn, you're a horse for strength," he said.

Darby studied the remaining logs. He shook his head wearily. "Do you have any ideas how I'm going to break those free?"

"Well, I been thinking and thinking. Trying to figure out the safest way. I come to the conclusion there ain't none. One of us going to have to swim for it. Start a couple hundred yards upriver and head for those pilings. If he could reach them, we'd string a rope across this side of the water. Tie it between the pilings and the nearest tree."

"And then what?"

"Then he could shinny up the pilings. 'Cause that's the only safe place out there."

Darby chuckled cryptically. "So, you're saying I should hop into that torrent, aim for the logs, and . . . if I make it, climb up the pilings. What, may I ask, is that going to accomplish?"

"Beats me. But you have to admit you'd be right on top of the problem. We sure ain't doing no good sitting over here on the bank looking at it."

"True. I wonder," he said slowly, "if I jumped up and down on the logs, would they break loose?"

"That's a hell of fine idea, Sheriff. Only, then what do you do?"

"Jump for the piling. As soon as I felt them start to move. I'd have a rope around my waist. Once I'd climbed those poles I could tie it down tight and pull myself across over the water."

"Why don't you just walk across the water?" Carson spat. "Be about as easy."

Darby stood up. "Unless you have a better solution, there is no choice."

Andy pulled his hat off and scratched his head. He looked worried.

"Why don't you get one of those young fellas to do it? You're the sheriff, so ask for volunteers, then order someone."

Darby removed his shirt and emptied his pockets. He hesitated, then reluctantly shed his pants. "Get a rope," he said. "Probably take three or four tied together. If I don't reach it, pull me in."

"Hell no! Don't do it. Find someone else."

"I can't," Darby said. "Besides, I'm the best man for the job. I outweigh anyone else out here by at least fifty pounds. And I may have to do some lifting to get those logs moving. Come on, let's get this over with."

Darby stood on the bank, judging the distance. He figured it to be about a hundred and fifty yards above the bridge. Behind him, Andy Carson and the others waited in silence. The talking was over now; nobody had any better suggestions. He tied the rope around his waist and waded in. The water was cold. Very cold, and dirty from spring runoff.

When it reached his chest, Darby felt himself losing footing. The current was swift and it lifted him away. He took a deep breath and started swimming. He aimed straight across, but for every foot he gained, the water carried him down-river at least five.

Darby was a strong swimmer and he chopped his hands into the water with cupped palms. He took five strokes before he lifted his head for air. The bridge was racing toward him. He had a long way to go before he was far enough out to reach the center. He took a deep breath and buried his face and swam with every ounce of strength he could muster. Another five strokes, and his face surfaced only long enough for air. Then he continued lashing out with his arms.

His heart thudded wildly. He felt his breath burning in his chest. Four strokes and he had to have air. He glanced sideways. The logs were just ahead. Faster! He struggled, his arms feeling like rock. The rope seemed to be pulling him down. He took two more strokes, felt the current slacken, then he struck the log.

It caught him in the side and knocked the breath out of him. Darby gasped for air and got water. He choked and grabbed blindly. His arms circled the rough bark of a log and he embraced it with his entire body. He felt his shin tearing on the bark, but most of all he felt himself being pulled under the log. He threw up a leg, somehow managed to get it hooked over the top. Then he battled, scraping, inching, tearing his way up and out of the water.

For a long minute he lay there inert, eyes closed, breath bursting in and out of his mouth. Over the roar of the current, he could hear distant shouts. He ignored them because he didn't have the strength to respond. And under his length, he felt the log rocking him like a baby.

His breathing slowed. Darby opened his eyes and coughed out a stomachful of river water. His fingernails were ripped and bloody, his entire length was scratched and crimson-streaked. But nothing was broken. Gingerly, he touched his chest, probed for a fractured rib. There was a pain when he lifted his arm, but he knew the place where he'd struck the log was just bruised. He was very lucky.

He twisted around and stared upriver. Suddenly, he wasn't so lucky. Between himself and the men on the bank, he could see that the rope passed under the log that jutted into the current. Almost holding his breath, Darby tugged. The rope resisted. He pulled again, harder. The log swayed. The rope held.

For a moment, he didn't move as the enormity of this unforeseen complication struck him. There had to be a solution! Darby calmed himself and studied the position of the rope and entanglement. The log that had trapped the rope was facing upstream, balanced at sixty-degree angle and wedged against the jam. If he pulled it hard enough, the rope might come free. It might also shift the log, send it arching into the current and then slamming into him.

Darby shivered. If that happened, it would strike with such force the other three logs would surely break free. And he'd go with them.

He reached down and fumbled at the knot at his waist. His fingers felt like exposed nerve ends. The knot was so tight he had to sit up and work at it with both hands. At last, he got it free. He dipped his hands back into the water and the pain became tolerable. Then he stood up, very slowly. Bent over, in a half crouch, he measured the distance to the pilings. Nine feet, no more. He calculated exactly where he would step covering the span.

Darby turned back to face upstream. He took the rope in both hands. Slowly, he began to apply pressure. The rope tightened and rose from the water. He pulled harder and the timber shifted. He could feel its near end grate against the log under his feet. Pull, man! Get it over!

He did. There was a grinding sound at his feet and the log underneath began to move. Upriver, the rope went slack and Darby saw the log twist, slowly, deliberately until it was broadside to the surging water. Then it started coming.

Darby dropped the rope and whirled around. He felt more than saw the logs underneath start to roll. He took three racing bounds and started to jump for the piling. The force of his weight turned the log and he didn't get the push-off he needed. His momentum carried him into the piling as an ear-splitting crack of wood rose in his ears.

Darby struck the piling at water level. He doubled his legs and grabbed it with all fours. Then he began to drag himself upward.

The first log that struck almost shook him free. He kept climbing. There was no time to look down. He knew he was barely out of the water. Another log struck, and the piling tilted under the blow. Then, almost instantly, they were gone. He clasped the piling to his chest and watched the four logs bouncing downriver in the white water.

Darby pressed his forehead against the wood and wondered, What now? My strength is gone. I can't hang here more than another minute. Why wait until I have nothing left?

He let loose and felt the cold river grab him, spin him around, and carry him away. Darby didn't fight the current this time. He began to swim almost as if he didn't care. Each stroke of his arms was merely a feeble slap.

But they added up, and almost a mile downriver, he felt his fingers touch mud and knew he'd made it. He was so weary he didn't even try to pull himself out. He just rolled over onto his back and closed his eyes.

Two days later, Darby was still in bed. He had a miserable cold and Dr. Sawyer had lectured him on the dangers of pneumonia. And he was a mass of scabs. The only skin that had escaped injury was his face. For that he was grateful.

"More tea, Darby, honey?"

He sneezed, blew his nose. "No, thank you, Dolly. How are they coming on the tree cutting?"

She plumped down on the bed beside him. "Andy Carson said they found a good stand less than two miles from the bridge. He said they'd get the trees felled today, trimmed tomorrow. After that, they'll start the hauling."

"Huh," Darby grunted. "You know the truth? I'm glad I'm here instead of out there swinging an ax all day. I hardly feel guilty at all."

"And you shouldn't." She leaned over and kissed him. "It's a real treat to have you all to myself and stuck in bed."

"Two more days and the doctor says I'll be able to help."

"Two more days is a long time," she purred. Her hand started to inch under the covers.

"Dolly . . . Dolly, my scabs!"

"Don't worry, I won't touch them. I—"

A loud knock sounded at the door.

"Damn," she breathed. "Maybe whoever it is will go away."

"Miss Beavers! Open up!"

Darby stiffened. "It's them!"

"Come on, we know you're in there. We could hear you talkin'. Bear and me don't want no trouble this time, ma'am. But we'll take the door if we have to."

"Where's your gun?" she hissed, jumping off the bed. "Where is it?"

"We're respectable now."

"Never! You'll never be respectable."

Darby blew his nose gustily. "You'd better open up. They won't leave by themselves."

"No gun?"

"No. Besides, I want to hear what they have to say. Maybe they've changed their minds and decided to leave Snakegrass."

"I guess it is worth finding out," Dolly admitted. She opened the door. Darby saw her stagger backward.

"What in the name—"

Zack pressed into the doorway. Bear was right behind. Darby jerked erect, not daring to believe what he saw.

They swept off their derbys. Zack jammed a thumb into his new vest pocket and struck a George Washington pose. "Well," he bounced, "I can see you're impressed. Slick as calf's slobber, ain't we?"

Darby stared at one, then the other. They were like a matched pair. Black suits, white shirts, black ties. Clean, pressed, immaculate. They'd even shaved and had their hair cut. They were transformed.

Dolly backed into a chair and plopped down. "I don't believe it," she whispered.

"Ha-ha," Bear laughed. "I see you didn't warn her."

"Nothing I might have said could have prepared Miss Beavers for this," Darby replied.

Their attention shifted back to Dolly. They seemed so coordinated Darby felt as if he were watching a puppet show. Zack cleared his throat. "We are pleased to come calling."

Bear took a step closer. "Both of us are."

"Calling!" Darby raged. "What do you mean?"

Zack ignored his outburst. His eyes softened, his voice lost its roughness. "We come to ask you to have supper with us—we'll pay. We're asking you, like gentlemen."

Darby's eyes rolled up and he sank back against his pillow. The entire affair *had* to be a bad dream. Close your eyes, man. Go back to sleep, and when you wake up again, none of this will have happened.

"Darby?" Her voice weak, pleading. "Darby, help! Don't you dare close your eyes and ignore me!"

He rolled his head sideways. "All right. Tell them no."

"Keep out of this," Zack warned.

"Darby, stay in that bed!" She turned back to them. "I—I appreciate your offer, but . . . but I can't."

"Well, why the hell not!" Bear swore. "He said we were buying. And he asked right, didn't he?"

"Of course, but . . . well, I'm not hungry."

"We can wait. We got business to do until you're hungry," Zack said stubbornly.

"What business?" Darby say upright.

Zack's chin stuck out belligerently. "I told you we was coming to talk to the folks in this town. We're going to personally invite them to move over to Snakegrass Junction. It's only fair they should have the first chance."

"The only response you'll get from this town is a bullet," Darby said bluntly.

"We aren't armed." Zack looked at Dolly. "Fact is, ma'am, we wanted to give you the first chance."

"To move over there? And give up this?"

"No offense, Miss Beavers, but our hotel is bigger and better than yours. We been trying to make do for the passengers, but you could do a sight more than us."

"Humph!" she snorted.

"It's a fact. For you, Bear and I have decided we'd offer a partnership. Course if you married one of us, we'd—"

"Married!" Dolly staggered back. "You're crazy!"

Zack's face reddened as though he'd been slapped. Darby turned his head away. He couldn't stand to see a proud man humiliated, no matter how justifiably. Maybe Dolly felt that way too, because he heard her say. "Listen, I'm sorry. You and Bear look very handsome in your new suits."

"You mean that?"

"Yes."

"Then, will you have supper with us?"

"I'm still not hungry. But you can do me a favor."

"Name it," they said together.

"Well, a lot of the townsfolk are out working on the bridge. If they return before you leave, I'm afraid there will be trouble."

"We ain't the kind to run," Bear said.

"Of course not. Only, you are unarmed. If they forced

things, you might have to fight. It would be a shame to see you ruin those new suits."

"She's got something there, Zack."

The tall man set his derby hat on his head. "I'm gonna honor your wishes. Like I told Buckingham, we didn't come seeking trouble. We come as businessmen with a proposition."

"You won't be welcomed," Darby said.

"Don't be so sure, city man. In fact, we'll drop on by after we've made the rounds and tell you how many folks are moving. And maybe then Miss Beavers will reconsider."

"Not a chance," Dolly said. "The Antelope Hotel is all I own in the world. I'm not leaving."

"There's always a chance," Zack drawled. "Be seeing you."

Darby watched them leave. "Well," he sighed, "you heard them. If anything, they're more convinced than ever that they'll own a town."

Dolly walked over to the window. "There they go, heading straight for Dooley's. You know, what scares me is that they might just pull it off."

"Dolly!"

"Well, it's possible. I'm around all day and I hear the talk. There are more than a few people who are considering leaving. Mostly, they're businessmen who are having a tough time. They're about to go under since the stage has rerouted."

"That will change soon."

She turned from the window and came to stand by his bed. "How can you be sure? There is no way you can guarantee that the Shoshone River Bridge won't be destroyed again."

"We'll post guards."

"They can't stay there forever. Oh, sure, you'll have plenty of volunteers the first few weeks, but after that. . . ."

"I know. But before that day comes I'm hoping this part of Wyoming will have seen the last of Mr. Ward, Zack Woolsey, and Bear Timberly."

"You won't believe this, but I almost like them. They were so . . . so sweet just now."

Darby shook his head. "Please, my dear, don't let them hear that or we'll never get rid of them."

Two hours later, Zack and Bear returned. "Well," Darby said. "I hope you are finally convinced of your folly."

"Nope," Zack replied. "In fact, me and Bear had some of these folks near talked into coming over."

"I don't believe it."

"Are you calling me a liar?" The threat was open, inviting. Darby was tempted. He could have thought of many things to call Zack, but, so far, liar wasn't one of them. He took a deep breath and let it out slowly. "No, I'm not. But I'd like to have a few names."

Bear sneered. "Don't tell him. He'll just go out and make it rough on those we talked to."

"He's right," Zack said. "We ain't telling. You'll know soon enough anyway." He glanced over at Dolly. "Be seeing you again. Soon. You change your mind, honey, you just give a whistle. He tries to stop you, we'll put a stop to him."

Then, before Darby could reply, Zack winked and they were gone.

"Blast and thunder!" Darby roared.

"Now, now. They didn't mean anything."

"Sure they did. I've got ears, woman!"

"They're bluffing. No one in Running Springs would leave."

Darby reached for a cigar. His thick eyebrows furrowed together. He lit the cigar and puffed quickly. "I wonder," he said. "I sure as the devil wonder."

CHAPTER 13

A half mile outside of town, Zack and Bear reined their horses into a stand of aspen and dismounted. Five minutes later, they emerged in their buckskins carrying rifles in one hand and suit boxes in the other.

"Damn," Bear swore. "It sure feels good to get back into our own duds again."

"For a fact. I wonder if we'll ever get used to wearing those suits? And I feel a heap better with our rifles. Don't know as how I ever want to go back to Running Springs unarmed again."

"Well, I sure don't," Bear said. "But at least we showed 'em we weren't scared."

"Yeah, but with all the men out at the bridge, there wasn't much to worry about." Zack glanced up at the sun. "We'd better ride. Those folks out at the river crossing will be coming back this way soon enough."

They remounted and continued east; their direction brought them almost exactly to the spot where Darby Buckingham had washed up two days earlier. A bend in the river prevented them from being seen by anyone working at the bridge. Both men placed their reins in their teeth. In one hand, they held aloft the boxed suits; in the other, their rifles. Heels drumming against their horses' sides, they entered the river and swam across.

On dry land, they stopped and dismounted. Zack tied his horse in the trees and motioned Bear to do the same. "Let's mosey up the river and have a peek. Ward will want to know how they're coming on the bridge."

Zack led the way, his long legs gliding him over the damp earth. Bear followed right behind. Though top-heavy and ponderous, he could move with almost as much stealth as his partner. It was something a hunter and trapper had to learn or he was useless.

"There it is," Zack said, dropping to his stomach behind a tree.

"I don't see anyone working."

"Me neither. Hell, they haven't even started." Zack smiled. "It looks good, Bear, damn good. At this rate we've got longer than I hoped."

"What do you suppose they're up to?"

"Probably off cutting logs. Up to now, I can't see that they've done much except clear away the ones we chopped up." Zack pursed his lips thoughtfully. "That was likely more work than I'd figured. I wish there was some way we could have leveled those pilings."

"There wasn't, Zack. You know that better'n I do. Those things are set to stay."

"Maybe. Maybe not. I do know one thing."

"What?"

"If we do it again, I'm going to figure out some way to flatten them."

Bear's face took on a troubled look. "But Ward says we won't have to. With all those letters he's sending, I thought—"

"Don't believe all the things he tells us. We're in for a battle. Buckingham and that town ain't about to roll over and play dead anytime soon. It might take months to strangle them into joining us."

"Months?"

"Well, maybe not that long," Zack hedged. He wasn't at all sure himself how long it would take Ward to convince the stage line to detour over to Snakegrass Junction. As far as Zack was concerned, it didn't matter. He'd destroy that bridge over and over until he whipped Running Springs. If he had to, he'd break their spirit. The decision was out of his hands. Only some rich man back East could put Snakegrass Junction back on the map. Until then, it was war.

"Cheer up, partner. Let Alvin S. Ward do the worrying. I don't much like him, but I figure he's a man who won't be beaten. So we'll just ride along on his wagon as far as we want to go, then we'll strike out on our own."

"Maybe," Bear said. "But don't forget that Buckingham said if the bridge got busted up again, he'd come over with a posse—and ropes."

"I ain't forgot. Neither has Ward. The two of us were talking about that just the other day. If we have to bust logs again, you know what Ward will do?"

"No."

"He'll send for a U.S. marshal a couple days before. By the time he'd get here the bridge would be gone, and when Buckingham and his men rode into Snakegrass the marshal'd be there to greet them."

"Why would a U.S. marshal take a stand for us?"

"He wouldn't take a stand," Zack explained. "But he'd have to ask for proof we done it. Buckingham wouldn't have any, so they couldn't touch us. Meantime we've bought another three or four weeks. Hell, man, just think! We could do it over and over. Make the law work for *us* after all these years."

Bear nodded thoughtfully. "It's downright awesome what a man can do when he puts his skull to it, ain't that so?"

"'Tis a fact for sure," Zack said solemnly. "Now, let's ride before the sun goes down and the mosquitoes attack."

During the following week, two more stages arrived in Snakegrass Junction loaded with passengers. Zack, Bear, and Alvin S. Ward worked hard to be perfect hosts. They polished their shooting exhibition and the Easterners loved it.

The three men labored from sunup to sundown. Bear and

Zack rose very early and went out hunting antelope and deer
for themselves and the passengers. Ward turned out to be an
exceptionally fine cook. During the week, forty gallons of
whitewash arrived and, in between stages, Bear and Zack
slopped great quantities along the store fronts. The town,
though an empty white shell, began to assume a bright, prom-
ising quality that the passengers did not miss.

On each eastward departing stage, Ward was careful to
send another packet of glowing letters praising the hospitality
of Snakegrass Junction. Many of the letters contained almost
identical phrases, dictated by Ward himself, extolling the vir-
tues of the food, the rooms, and of course, the tasteful
magnificence of The Great Whiskey Palace.

On the following Tuesday, the stage brought a letter from
the stage company. Alvin S. Ward, forever playing the man
of retirement and dignity, lost control. He let out a whoop
and ran for The Great Whiskey Palace, waving the letter
overhead and shouting. "Bear, Zack, hurry! This may be it!"

The three men gathered over a table. Ward took a deep
breath and expelled it slowly. He opened the letter and read
it aloud.

Dear Proprietors of Snakegrass Junction:

*I take this opportunity to extend our Company's
thanks for the excellent hospitality which you have been
providing our passengers. Really, the number of letters
we are beginning to receive is quite extraordinary.*

*As you know, our Company's business depends on
passenger satisfaction. I am aware that Snakegrass Junction was our original stage stop. Personally, I opposed
the past decision to circumvent your town. Had such a
move not been made, we would not presently be having
trouble at the Shoshone River Crossing.*

*It is my intention to present these highly laudatory
letters at our next board meeting. I am confident you
will continue to provide exemplary accommodations for*

our passengers and that I can gain a more permanent ar-
rangement for Snakegrass Junction.

                    Sincerely,
                    William Winthrope

P.S. Word is reaching us that you have two outstanding
old hunters who are providing quite a show. I, myself,
would be interested in witnessing such a performance.
Also, I would like to know if an acquaintance, a Mr.
Darby Buckingham, is staying in your area. If so, please
ask him to write regarding a possible story idea based on
our stage line.

"Holy hog horns!" Zack bellowed. "We did it!"

"Wahoo!" Bear yelled. He grabbed Zack by the arm and
they joined in a particularly wild jig usually reserved for the
very last stages of a monumental drunk.

Alvin S. Ward, however, remained bent over the letter, a
thoughtful look on his face. At last, Zack disengaged himself
from Bear. He was out of breath and filled with a wild sense
of triumph. They *had* done it. He could scarcely believe
their good fortune.

Without asking, he reached over the bar and fished a bottle
from the counter. He took a long drink and handed the whiskey to Bear. "This calls for a celebration! Hey, Ward, come
on over and join us."

"Maybe later."

Zack shook his head and stiffly walked over to the table.
"What the hell is wrong with you? Dammit, man, you look
about as happy as a cat in water. We won, didn't we?"

He looked up and said, "Perhaps."

"Hey, Bear, he says we ain't won yet. Better bring the
whiskey over here and let's find out what he ain't told us."

They sat down. Zack leaned forward. "We don't like to be
kept guessing, Ward. Now, either you didn't read it right the
first time or you left out the bad parts. Which was it?"

"Neither. I'll tell you what's bothering me: Darby Buckingham."

"We can handle him," Bear said.

Ward ignored the statement and continued. "The letter
says we're supposed to ask Buckingham to contact this Mr.
Winthrope. Gentlemen, that's the problem."

"I think I see," Zack said. "You're afraid he'll write the big
man and explain what we're up to in Snakegrass. That seems
simple enough: we just say nothing."

"Uh-uh. That would be very unwise. This Winthrope
wasn't *suggesting* we contact Buckingham, he was *telling* us
to."

Zack took a pull on the bottle. "We could stall until the
stage line stops here permanent."

"But how long will that be, dammit! What if Winthrope
gets suspicious in the meantime? What," his voice dropped,
"if Buckingham himself writes this man?"

"I guess we'll just have to take our chances," Zack said,
studying Ward intently for a reaction. "There isn't much we
can do about it, is there?"

A look of amusement crossed Ward's face. "Don't seem
like. But, still, I always make it a point to understand anyone
who might oppose me. What do you know about him?"

"Well, he's a dude and no good at all with a gun. I guess he
only took the sheriff's job until Cather is back on his feet."

"He sounds very incompetent."

"Not altogether. You'd be surprised at how strong he is.
Bear will back me up on that. The two of us had a tussle with
him up in the Antelope Hotel and he's a rough man to bring
down."

"Sneaky, too," Bear added. "Caught me with a couple
punches I never even seen."

"Is that right? He looks . . . well, kind of soft."

"He ain't," Zack said. "Under his lard there's a whole lot
of muscle."

Ward changed the conversation. "I would never fight him. Tell me, besides the sheriff, does he have any close friends? Perhaps a woman."

"Yeah, he's got one of those," Zack said. "The best-looking gal in the whole town. Make you drool watching her."

Ward chuckled. "And I can tell by your voice you've watched her quite a bit."

"Can't figure what she sees in him," Bear said. "Hell, we even asked her out to supper when we was in our new suits. Tried everything, but she wouldn't go."

Zack said glumly, "We never had much practice with that kind. I thought sure I was doing things right, but we got nothing."

"Perhaps, gentlemen, she loves the man."

"She couldn't!" Zack was surprised at his own outburst. He frowned and studied his hands thoughtfully. "We offered her a partnership in our hotel if she'd come over."

"Wasn't that . . ." Ward hesitated. "Wasn't that a bit generous?"

"Nope. You see, she owns and runs the Antelope Hotel, and me and Bear figured she could be a real help overseeing our place. You know, it looks sorta funny having two hunters like us changing linen and such. If we could just get her to come on over, we'd have the best hotel between here and San Francisco."

"I believe you would at that," Ward said. "There ought to be some way of changing the lady's mind."

"Now I don't think so. Me and Bear gave it our best try. She was in Buckingham's room when we made our pitch."

"Wait a minute. You say she was in his room? Doing what?"

"Hell, who knows? He was lying in bed and—"

"Well," he said with a golden-toothed smile.

"Well, what?"

"That explains it, Zack. She was probably afraid to accept

your offer, because he was there. Could be she's scared to leave him."

Zack thought on it for a minute. He wanted to believe Ward. To his mind, it was the only reason that could possibly account for her refusal. But he wasn't sure. Buckingham didn't seem the type to beat a woman. And Dolly Beavers didn't seem much like the kind to let a man buffalo her.

"Look, I know what you're thinking," Ward persisted. "But you admit you haven't had much experience with that type of woman. So it may come as a shock when I tell you that just as often as not good women are taken advantage of. It's true! You offered her a chance to escape that wretched fate. To move to a new town. To be a partner. She must realize that her hotel will become worthless when the stage no longer brings in passengers. Unless I miss my bet she really wanted to accept your offer."

Bear looked sideways. "Zack?" He also wanted to believe Ward. It showed on his face.

"I don't know what we can do about it," Zack said finally.

Ward groaned. "Gentlemen. Do my ears deceive me? Could you possibly be serious! No. There is," he said leaning across the table, "one sure way to find out."

"Ask her again?"

"No! Rescue her."

"Give me that bottle," Zack said. He took a long drink. Then he looked Ward square in the eye. "And what if she don't want to be rescued?"

"Do it anyway. There is nothing, absolutely nothing a good woman wants and dreams about more than to be rescued. Ah, to be sure, she may not show it—at first. Why, she may kick and fight and resist for days, but don't you see?"

"See what?"

"She has to. No self-respecting woman would allow herself to be rescued without a fuss. But, believe me, deep down she'll thank you for it to her dying day. She will . . . she will love you forever!"

"Which one?" Bear stammered.

"That is not mine to see. The lady's heart secretes the answer."

"Whew," Zack breathed. "I had no idea." He leaned his head back and gazed at the ceiling. "As near as I can figure, there's only one big hitch to this whole rescue idea."

"Don't tell me you're worried about reprisal?"

"Who the hell is he?" Bear growled.

Ward said patiently, "You're worried that Buckingham and the whole town will come after you."

"That's right," Zack said. "Miss Beavers is awful friendly with 'most everyone. If you think we've caused a stir by busting up their bridge, . . ." His words trailed off. The message was clear.

"I know of a way," he said quietly.

"How?"

"A letter. A simple letter left in her room stating that she has gone of her own free will and knows an opportunity when she sees one. We can even add that she hopes others will relocate their businesses to Snakegrass. If she's as influential and well regarded as you say, her note will carry a great deal of weight."

"Damn," Bear whispered. "It would work, Zack."

Zack thought about it. He ignored the tugging on his arm by Bear and focused on Ward's eyes. They matched his own without wavering. Why won't it work? he thought. After all, a few weeks ago who would have believed they'd own a town?

Almost involuntarily, he nodded. "Write the letter. If she don't want to stay after being here with us for a week, she can go back. It would just prove she's all looks and no brains. We'd not want her anyway."

"I think I still would," Bear said.

Zack shot him a disgusted look. "She'll not be touched by either of us until . . . how did you put that?"

"Only her heart secretes the answer," Ward repeated.

"Yeah. So write the letter. Then we're on our way, tonight."

"Why tonight? Why not now, while Buckingham and the others are out of town working on the bridge?"

Zack grinned. "Why not! Write the letter and we'll go right now."

Alvin S. Ward jumped up and hurried into the back room, where he slept. He emerged seconds later with a blank sheet of paper and pen. "It's a shame you boys never learned to read or write."

"The hell with that," Zack said. "The lacking ain't hurt us a lick 'til now."

"That's nice to know." He picked up the pen and began to write, composing his words with the greatest care.

Buckingham:
   We tuk yore woman. If ya want her back yull have to pruve yore man enouf to do it on yore own. Come alone to Snakegrass an we will settle onct and forall who is going to have her. No triks. We'll be waitin.

Zack studied it carefully, then showed it to Bear. "It looks like it'll do. I'll be damned sure to put it where the sheriff sees it."

"Do that," Ward said gravely. "Make real sure you do that."

They circled in from the north where the Tetons were skirted with heavy forest. Where the trees opened into Running Springs, Zack had decided to go ahead on foot. It was midafternoon, and business activity was almost nonexistent. Nevertheless, the two hunters stalked the town, missing not a single covering tree, rock, or bush. So stealthily did they move, they passed two sleeping dogs by less than ten feet. Their journey ended at the back of the Antelope Hotel.

This was a familiar routine for them, and they had spoken no words but communicated only in gestures. Though never bothered with words, it was understood that Zack was the leader and, as such, it was his responsibility to make the decisions. Bear trusted him completely. Zack had never failed to get them to the best spot for shooting. More than once, he had led them safely through hostile Indian country.

So, as they pressed close to the rear of the hotel, there was no discussion and Bear waited patiently while Zack studied his next move.

Zack saw a shed attached to the rear of the building. Perhaps used for storage, possibly part of the kitchen, it was small and windowless. There was a heavy lock on the door. Zack frowned. He didn't want to fight the lock. He had no idea how it even worked. But, somehow, he knew that going around to the front was too risky. Even if they did manage to slip in undetected, they would never make it with Dolly. He had the feeling they'd have to take her out feet first.

Zack's eyes lifted to the roof of the shed. It was low, only about seven feet high. Above, the second-story windows were another twelve feet. It could be done. He turned to Bear and motioned with an upward rolling of his hands. Bear showed no reaction. Only, his chin dipped a fraction. They started forward.

An open water barrel stood full and sweating nearby. It was huge and solid with four iron bands. Zack glanced at it and Bear moved quickly. He reached down and pressed his hands against the staves. Slowly it came off the ground, leaving a dark wet circle in the dirt covered with pale, blind bugs. Bear straightened with the barrel rocking slightly between his thick legs. He swayed forward, the muscles corded in his face and neck. Five steps and he eased the barrel back to earth.

Zack noted with awe that the water barely lopped the sides. He placed a steadying hand on Bear's shoulder and hopped up, feet planted on the rim. It was an easy jump to the roof and he motioned down at Bear to follow.

Zack moved quickly now. If someone happened to enter the alley the alarm would be sounded. He stood under the window and Bear knelt down. Zack stepped onto his shoulders and felt himself being raised against the wall. When his eyes reached window level, he peered inside between the curtains. He let his breath out slowly. The room was vacant. Dolly's and Buckingham's rooms were across the hall, fronting Main Street. Probably, he thought, she rented the ones in front first.

"A mite higher," he whispered. He lifted the window sash and looked down. "Stay somewheres out of sight until I bring her to the window. Then come back up and help us down."

"Be careful, Zack. She lets out just one holler and the whole town will come running."

Zack jumped up and got his chest inside and then dropped silently into the room. He peered back down at his friend. "If that should happen, you streak outa here fast."

"You go to hell, Zack."

He laughed softly. "Only if you ride in with me. This shouldn't take long. Be back in a few minutes."

At the hallway door, Zack poked his head out and made sure no one was around. Then he tiptoed down to Dolly's room and knocked softly.

"Who is it?"

"Me, Zack Woolsey. Open up. I want to talk to you."

Inside, the room became quiet. Zack clasped the door handle and decided to give her one more chance before he broke through. "It's about Buckingham."

"What about him?" The voice was close.

"He may be in danger."

The lock turned and she started to open it. Zack shoved his weight, hard. He barreled in and crashed into her. Then both fell on the carpet. Dolly thrashed wildly. He saw a scream rise in her throat and clamped his hand over her mouth. "Listen," he snapped, "I come to rescue you."

Her eyes widened. Her muffled voice sounded angry. A fist came up and cracked him against the side of the head. Zack swore. She wasn't going for it at all.

"Aw, for Chrissakes," he sighed. "I didn't want it to come to this." He reached around and drew out his bowie knife.

Dolly's eyes grew so round with fear that he couldn't bear to look at her. As he lifted the knife, another scream pressed its way against his palm. One-handed, Zack flipped the knife around and snapped her smartly on the head. Dolly went limp.

"Blamed if that ain't going to give Bear a running start on me," he said, rising. Quickly, he slipped outside and down the hallway until he reached Darby Buckingham's room. Then he yanked the letter out of his shirt pocket and shoved it under the door. "He won't miss that."

When he returned to her room, she was still out cold. There was no time to waste. If he could have, Zack would have liked to take some of her things along. A few dresses, some frilly things she'd like. He had the feeling she'd miss woman's stuff. He glanced over at her dressing table. Without bothering to choose by smell, he grabbed a handful of small bottles and stuffed them into his pockets. At least she could smell good.

She was heavier than he'd expected. Lacking Bear's strength, Zack felt his long, slender legs quiver under her weight. He poked his head out the door and took a quick peek. All clear. He stepped out and kicked the door shut. A moment later he was at the rear window.

Bear materialized in the alley and was immediately waiting

with outstretched arms. Zack set her carefully on the sill. Feet first or head first? Head first. He got an arm under her neck and eased her over backward.

For one awful moment, he lost his grip. Dolly's head bounced against the wall with a loud "Thunk." Oh God, Zack thought, I sure hope I haven't killed her. He wrapped an arm around her dress and leaned out the window as far as he dared.

Below, he saw Bear reach up and grab her. Zack caught a glimpse of the expression on Bear's face. Total, absolute disgust. Zack looked away bleakly and continued to ease her down. Finally, he had her by the ankles. Honor prevented him from peeking. It wouldn't be fair. She was a lady.

At last they had her on the roof. Bear returned to the wall and Zack came down. Bear's face was murderous. "What did you do to her!" he hissed.

"Later. I had no choice. Let's get off the roof and get out of here. Is she all right?"

"She's got knots on her skull but she's breathin'. Zack, you shouldn't oughta have—"

"Later!" Zack hurried over to the edge. "Stand on the barrel and I'll lift her down to you."

"Hope you're better'n last time," he grunted.

Bear reached up and Zack lowered her down. Suddenly, there was a loud cracking noise. Bear's mouth formed a round circle. Then they dropped as a great whoosh of water exploded in the alley. Zack closed his eyes and then forced them open. Bear was sitting on his rump with Dolly still in his arms. The barrel staves lay out around him like a peeled onion. The area was flooded.

Zack bit back a grin. Not now, he told himself. Bear will kill you if you so much as show a single tooth. Zack hopped to the ground and glanced up and down the back alley. "Let's get out of here. You can take a bath later."

He heard a strangled noise but he didn't look back. Bear

couldn't catch him, toting Miss Beavers. And by the time they got back to their horses he'd be over the worst of it. All in all, Zack thought, ducking and running for a tree, they hadn't done badly. Now everything depended on the woman.

CHAPTER 14

Darby Buckingham rode into Running Springs with weariness running like a current through his bones. But they'd made good progress and the last of the timbers were cut and ready to be placed. No one had quite figured how they were going to do it, but somehow they would. And quickly. Every day the bridge was down was another day Running Springs died. For all practical purposes, business had ceased.

He unsaddled the black gelding and put it in the corral. As Darby trudged toward the Antelope Hotel, the sun was just sinking under the prairie. The sight was beautiful and, ordinarily, he would have lit a cigar and watched it. But, this evening, he was out of cigars and too damned tired.

Nearing the hotel, he realized Dolly hadn't been waiting for him as usual. Perhaps she had also had a rough day, though it was hard to imagine why. Since the stage stopped coming, Dolly's hotel business was nothing.

Darby labored up the stairs and started down the hallway. He paused at Dolly's door, then passed on. He needed a glass of brandy and a bath before company.

The note was folded off center. That was his first impression as he bent to pick it up. He closed the door and deposited his body on the bed. Then he read the note. His breathing quickened.

He read the note again, his mouth twisting into a terrible grimace. The note fell between his feet unnoticed. "You fools!" he rasped hoarsely, "I gave you every chance to remain free men. I even underwent the personal ridicule and anger of the town I have sworn to protect for your wild, worthless sakes. But this time you have gone too far!"

Darby strode to his dresser. He removed the derringer and shoved it into his pocket. Then he left. At the entrance to her room, Darby tried the knob, found it locked, and hurled himself against the door, taking it off the wall. He shot a quick glance around, saw nothing out of place, and left.

He made one stop. At the Sheriff's Office, he rummaged in the desk until he found Zeb Cather's badge. He pinned it to his coat, feeling a little silly. Maybe it was superstitious to think that the badge might bring him luck. But, silly or not, if he took a bullet, he wanted to die wearing it. He grabbed the shotgun from the gun rack, checked the load, and headed for the livery.

Darby wasn't sure what he'd say or do when he got to Snakegrass Junction. But Zack and Bear had committed kidnaping. Forcible abduction. Maybe, he thought bleakly, much more. For such a crime they'd go to prison—or the cemetery.

He didn't remember the ride to Snakegrass Junction. He traveled the distance with his mind in a swirling tempest. Even swimming the Shoshone River in darkness brought no memory. It was only when he came to the edge of town that Darby Buckingham seemed to emerge from the spell that held him.

He reined the black gelding in at the end of the street and dismounted. There was just one building whose lights cast a glow onto the ground in front of it. It was The Great Whiskey Palace. He could hear no sound coming from inside. They waited. His first thought was to go in from the rear alley. But after a moment's consideration, he rejected the idea as impractical. It would be pitch black and the chances of finding the correct door to The Great Whiskey Palace were remote. No, he decided, better to go in fast. They'd be ready, he was sure of that, but such actions were decided by a split-second. With the shotgun, he had a chance.

He began to walk down the street, placing his feet as lightly as possible. What if they were holding her before them? Using her as a shield?

That stopped him still in his tracks. Sweat beaded across his forehead. It was something to consider. He would have to hesitate before firing. There went his split-second advantage.

He was almost there. Darby changed direction and eased his weight onto the boardwalk. He crept forward and flattened himself against the wall. Then he craned his neck around and peered through the front window. He saw them.

Bear and Zack sat alone. A nearly empty whiskey bottle stood on the table between them. The two men were leaning forward talking. They were too far toward the back for Darby to be able to understand their conversation.

Darby scanned the room, missing nothing. Where was Dolly? And Alvin S. Ward? He faded away from the window, a troubled expression on his face. What if she were hurt? Or dead? Why else wouldn't she be with them! He could not bear to wait another instant. He had to know.

Pulling the gun up to his chest, Darby launched himself past the window and crashed through the swinging doors. There was a yell and he caught the image of Bear and Zack flying for their rifles. He slammed the shotgun to his shoulder and yelled, "Don't move or I'll shoot!"

Zack and Bear had acted swiftly. They were in a tangle on the floor, but their rifles were aiming at him. "Drop them!" he repeated.

They stared like wild animals trapped in a dark corner. Darby sighted down the shotgun, his finger tightening on both triggers. The buffalo rifles pointed back at him like long fingers of death. One last chance, he thought, then I'll open up before it's too late.

"I said drop those rifles!"

"Go to hell," Zack rumbled. "You'll be as dead as we will!"

"Where is she?"

"Upstairs. Ward just went to check on her."

Darby wanted to glance up. Wanted to as bad as he'd ever wanted to do anything in his life. There was a balcony up there. He remembered it from the last time. But he dared not look, because that's when they'd kill him.

His voice sounded foreign. "Is she . . . alive?"

"Yeah. But you ain't taking her back. And we ain't letting you see her. So," Zack hissed, "do what you come to do."

Darby swallowed. His mind reeled. Something was wrong. If they'd kidnapped Dolly to bait him into a trap, why—

"Kill him! Kill him! What are you waiting for!"

Out of the corner of his eye, Darby caught a glimpse of movement. Up, to the right on the balcony. A shot banged into the room and a bullet ate wood beside him on the bar top. A woman screamed and Darby could wait no longer. He pulled the shotgun up and the roar of his gun exploded at the form. Ward yelled and spun around against the wall. He reeled back to the balcony railing and raised his gun. One arm dangled redly. Darby had the terrible feeling he couldn't miss. There was no choice. No time to think. Again he fired. The blast and smoke momentarily filled Darby's senses. He staggered sideways. Looking up, he saw Alvin S. Ward spread-eagled against the wall. The gold teeth were locked in agony; then he fell.

"Darby, look out!"

He saw Dolly and knew what she meant. It was just too damn late to matter. He twisted around and faced Zack and Bear with empty shotgun. He knew he was as good as dead. In a last, futile effort, Darby dropped his weapon and grabbed for the derringer in his pocket. It was halfway free when Zack pulled the trigger.

Darby felt a scalding pain in his fingers and the derringer was gone.

"Please!" Dolly shouted. "Don't kill him. Kill me first!"

The three men's heads snapped up. Dolly was leaning over the railing. Her hands were clasped together and her eyes were squeezed shut. She was a shrine—a prayer in human form.

Zack whispered, "Put it down, Bear. It's over."

Bear's gun thudded on the wooden floor and the spell was broken. Dolly opened her eyes and whirled away from the railing. They watched her race down the staircase, cross the saloon floor, and throw herself into Darby Buckingham's arms.

Zack and Bear couldn't seem to stand the sight. They passed by, their eyes averted. But, before they reached the door, Zack reached over and grabbed two bottles of whiskey. Without a word, Darby watched them leave as he held Dolly Beavers to his chest and let her cry.

Alone in The Great Whiskey Palace, she was able to tell him what had happened. The note he showed her was Alvin S. Ward's. He had set them up. In one, final showdown, Ward had intended to be the only survivor. And it had almost worked.

"So that explains it," Darby said. "Why they weren't waiting for me or using you for protection. They didn't know I was coming. They didn't know."

Dolly brushed tears from her face. "They thought they were rescuing me from you. They kept saying I had nothing more to fear. You couldn't hurt me. I . . . I tried to explain, but they wouldn't listen. Finally, I started screaming and they left. It wasn't long afterwards that he," she said glancing up at the balcony, "he came in and told me to shut up or he'd kill me."

"Then, I suppose, he waited for me to arrive."

"Yes. He thought you would come in shooting. You didn't. He had to play it out. He'd gone too far to turn back."

"What about them?" Darby asked.

"Please," she said, "let them alone. They were tricked into believing they were doing what was right. I won't say I was taken by force. I'll swear I went of my own free will."

Darby smiled. "Dolly, I've never seen you look more beautiful. Now we'd better go have a talk with them. Before I leave, I'll have their promise that they'll quit this town."

She nodded. "Let me see your hand. Look, it's barely hurt. Do me a favor?"

"Of course."

"When you talk to them, just remember they could have killed you—and they might have had all of this." She studied the room and shook her head sadly. "This is so beautiful it almost makes me understand why Alvin S. Ward never abandoned it. Why he did what he did."

"Come on," Darby said, "and I'll remember."

The two hunters were sitting on the boardwalk. They looked beaten, and old. Zack cleared his throat. "Well, that's it, then. I can't blame you for ordering us to leave." He shook his head sadly. "But . . . but you don't know how Bear and me feel. It was our town. You know . . . to those passengers we were somebody. Never had that feeling before. Sorta hard to give up."

Despite all the resolution he could muster, Darby felt himself going soft with sympathy. He was listening to a couple of crazy old men who had caused him more trouble than he dared remember. But they'd spared his life only minutes before and they'd never lied to him. And Zack, he knew, wasn't lying now.

"But what the hell," Zack was saying. "Canada ain't so bad. We kinda hoped to settle down and find us wives someday. Guess we was fools to think any woman would have us."

I

"That's not true!" Dolly protested. "There are plenty of women who would be proud to marry you. Good ones that are lonely like you."

"That right?" Bear said, suddenly all interest.

"Of course. There are several lovely widows right in Running Springs."

"Dolly," Darby cautioned, an edge creeping into his voice.

"Naw," Zack shrugged. "It ain't our way to live off anyone. So I guess we'll be riding. But, before we do, we'll help you fix the bridge. Sure hate to see this town die, though. Especially The Great Whiskey Palace."

Suddenly, a shiver seemed to travel up Zack's spine. He leapt to his feet. "I got it!" he yelled. "Once we fix the bridge, we'll *move* the Whiskey Palace to Running Springs!"

"No, uh, you can't do that," Darby stammered.

"Sure they can," Dolly laughed.

Zack grabbed his bottle and raced headlong down the street. He skidded to a halt before the great saloon. They saw him tilt his head at a measuring angle.

"Zack and Bear's Whiskey Palace," he yelled down the street to them. "Hey, Bear! Get the paint. Buckingham, you can write it on the sign for us. We'll move this place board by board! Be finished by winter."

"Yahoo!" Bear hollered, running into the hotel for what Darby guessed would be a paint can and brush.

"Look out, you widow women!" Zack yelled.

"Hey, Buckingham, come on! Show me how you'll write it."

Darby dropped his head into his hands and moaned. He felt Dolly's arms encircle him. "Cheer up," she laughed sweetly. "Zeb Cather will be sheriff again by winter. And they'll give you plenty to write about."

Another moan. It was as much of an answer as he could summon.